JOEL WHITBURN PRESENTS

1

POP 3/24/45-3/13/04

R&B 1/30/65-3/13/04

COUNTRY 1/11/64-3/13/04

ALBUM PIX

FULL COLOR

Billboard.

Chart Data Compiled From *Billboard's* Pop, R&B and Country Album Charts, 1945-2004.

ISBN 0-89820-158-6

Record Research Inc.
P.O. Box 200
Menomonee Falls, Wisconsin 53052-0200 U.S.A.

Phone: (262) 251-5408
Fax: (262) 251-9452
E-Mail: books@recordresearch.com
Web Site: www.recordresearch.com

CONTENTS

The
#1 Pop
Albums
1945-2004

This section displays, in chronological order, full-color representations of the 691 albums that hit #1 on *Billboard's* Pop Albums chart from March 24, 1945 through March 13, 2004. The chart is currently named The Billboard 200.

The date an album first hit #1 is listed below each album's picture. The total weeks the album held the #1 position is listed to the right of the date.

Billboard has not published an issue for the last week of the year since 1976. For the years 1976 through 1991, *Billboard* considered the charts listed in the last published issue of the year to be "frozen" and all chart positions remained the same for the unpublished week. This frozen chart data is included in our tabulations. Since 1992, *Billboard* has compiled The Billboard 200 chart for the last week of the year, even though an issue is not published. This chart is only available through *Billboard's* Web site or by mail. Our tabulations include this unpublished chart data.

3/24/45 - 12
The King Cole Trio...
The King Cole Trio

4/14/45 - 2
Song of Norway...*Original Cast*

5/12/45 - 16
Glenn Miller...*Glenn Miller*

8/11/45 - 6
Carousel...*Original Cast*

9/15/45 - 5
Freddie Slack's Boogie Woogie...
Freddie Slack

10/20/45 - 6
Going My Way...
Bing Crosby/Soundtrack

12/1/45 - 6
On The Moon-Beam...
Vaughn Monroe

12/8/45 - 6
Merry Christmas...
Bing Crosby

2/23/46 - 4
State Fair...*Dick Haymes*

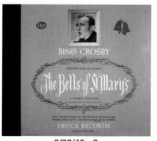

3/23/46 - 2
The Bells Of St. Mary's...
Bing Crosby/Soundtrack

4/6/46 - 7
The Voice of Frank Sinatra...
Frank Sinatra

5/25/46 - 3
Benny Goodman Sextet Session...
Benny Goodman

7/20/46 - 4
Dancing In The Dark...
Carmen Cavallaro

8/17/46 - 4
King Cole Trio, Volume 2...
The King Cole Trio

8/31/46 - 2
a Cole Porter review...
David Rose and his Orchestra

9/28/46 - 7
Ink Spots...*Ink Spots*

11/16/46 - 1
Merry Christmas Music...
Perry Como

11/23/46 - 7
Merry Christmas...*Bing Crosby*

1/11/47 - 1
All-Time Favorites by Harry James...
Harry James

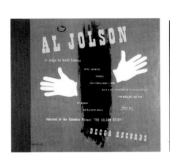

2/1/47 - 25
Al Jolson in songs he made famous...*Al Jolson*

8/2/47 - 5
Dorothy Shay (The Park Avenue Hillbillie) Sings...*Dorothy Shay*

8/16/47 - 10
Al Jolson Souvenir Album...
Al Jolson

1947 / 1948

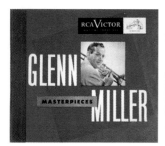

11/8/47 - 6
Glenn Miller Masterpieces...
Glenn Miller

11/15/47 - 8
Merry Christmas...*Bing Crosby*

1/24/48 - 1 — **Dorothy Shay (The Park Avenue Hillbillie) Goes To Town...***Dorothy Shay*

2/28/48 - 3
A Sentimental Date With Perry...
Perry Como

3/20/48 - 2
St. Patrick's Day...
Bing Crosby

4/3/48 - 6
Down Memory Lane...
Vaughn Monroe

5/15/48 - 1
Busy Fingers...*The Three Suns*

5/22/48 - 1
Song Hits of 1932...*Songs Of Our Times/Carmen Cavallaro*

5/29/48 - 8 — **A Presentation Of Progressive Jazz...**
Stan Kenton And His Orchestra

7/24/48 - 14
Al Jolson - Volume Three...
Al Jolson

10/16/48 - 3
Theme Songs...
Various Artists

11/20/48 - 9
Merry Christmas...*Bing Crosby*

1/22/49 - 2
Vaughn Monroe Sings...
Vaughn Monroe

1/29/49 - 1
Roses In Rhythm...
Frankie Carle

2/12/49 - 6
Words And Music...
Soundtrack

3/19/49 - 10
Kiss Me, Kate...*Original Cast*

6/4/49 - 69
South Pacific...*Original Cast*

12/24/49 - 3
Merry Christmas...*Bing Crosby*

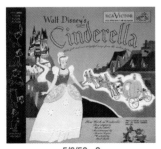

5/6/50 - 2
Cinderella...*Soundtrack*

5/13/50 - 12 — Young Man With A
Horn...*Doris Day and Harry*
James/Soundtrack

7/22/50 - 3 — Ralph Flanagan plays
Rodgers & Hammerstein II for
dancing...*Ralph Flanagan*

8/12/50 - 8
Annie Get Your Gun...
Soundtrack

9/30/50 - 11
Three Little Words...
Soundtrack

12/16/50 - 5
Merry Christmas...*Bing Crosby*

2/24/51 - 6
The Toast Of New Orleans...
Mario Lanza/Soundtrack

3/17/51 - 1
Guys And Dolls...*Original Cast*

4/7/51 - 6
Voice Of The Xtabay...
Yma Sumac

4/21/51 - 3
Lullaby Of Broadway...
Doris Day/Soundtrack

6/2/51 - 10
The Great Caruso...
Mario Lanza/Soundtrack

8/11/51 - 19
Show Boat...*Soundtrack*

12/22/51 - 3
**Mario Lanza sings Christmas
songs**...*Mario Lanza*

1/12/52 - 16
An American In Paris...
Soundtrack

3/15/52 - 4
I'll See You In My Dreams...
Doris Day/Soundtrack

5/3/52 - 25
With A Song In My Heart......
Jane Froman/Soundtrack

10/18/52 - 4
The Merry Widow...
Soundtrack

10/25/52 - 2
Liberace at the piano...
Liberace

11/1/52 - 15
I'm In The Mood For Love...
Eddie Fisher

11/15/52 - 4
Because You're Mine...
Mario Lanza/Soundtrack

12/20/52 - 8 — 1937/38 Jazz Concert
No. 2...*Benny Goodman*

1953

1/3/53 - 1
Christmas With Eddie Fisher...
Eddie Fisher

2/14/53 - 17
Hans Christian Andersen...
Danny Kaye/Soundtrack

2/21/53 - 2
Stars And Stripes Forever...
Soundtrack

1953 / 1954 / 1955

4/4/53 - 23
Music For Lovers Only...
Jackie Gleason

4/18/53 - 1
Arthur Godfrey's TV Calendar
Show...*Arthur Godfrey*

6/6/53 - 2
The Music of Victor Herbert...
Mantovani

12/26/53 - 2 — Christmas With
Arthur Godfrey And All The Little
Godfreys...*Arthur Godfrey*

1954

3/6/54 - 1
Tawny...*Jackie Gleason*

3/13/54 - 10
The Glenn Miller Story...
Soundtrack

3/20/54 - 11 — Glenn Miller Plays
Selections From The Film "The
Glenn Miller Story"...*Glenn Miller*

8/21/54 - 42 — The Student Prince
and other great musical
comedies...*Mario Lanza*

10/30/54 - 4
Music, Martinis, and Memories...
Jackie Gleason

1955

5/28/55 - 2
Crazy Otto...*Crazy Otto*

6/11/55 - 6
Starring Sammy Davis, Jr....
Sammy Davis, Jr.

6/25/55 - 4
in the Wee Small Hours...
Frank Sinatra

7/23/55 - 19
Love Me Or Leave Me...
Doris Day/Soundtrack

7/23/55 - 2
Lonesome Echo...*Jackie Gleason*

1956

1/28/56 - 4
Oklahoma!...*Soundtrack*

3/24/56 - 6
Belafonte...*Harry Belafonte*

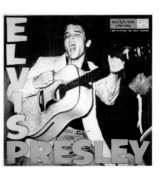

5/5/56 - 10
Elvis Presley...*Elvis Presley*

7/14/56 - 15
My Fair Lady...*Original Cast*

9/8/56 - 31
Calypso...*Harry Belafonte*

10/6/56 - 1
The King And I...
Soundtrack

10/13/56 - 1
The Eddy Duchin Story...
Carmen Cavallaro/Soundtrack

12/8/56 - 5
Elvis...*Elvis Presley*

5/27/57 - 8
Love Is The Thing...
Nat "King" Cole

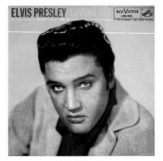

7/22/57 - 10
Around The World In 80 Days...
Soundtrack

7/29/57 - 10
Loving You...
Elvis Presley/Soundtrack

12/16/57 - 4
Elvis' Christmas Album...
Elvis Presley

12/30/57 - 1
Merry Christmas...*Bing Crosby*

1/20/58 - 2
Ricky...*Ricky Nelson*

2/10/58 - 5
Come Fly with me...
Frank Sinatra

3/17/58 - 12
The Music Man...*Original Cast*

5/19/58 - 31
South Pacific...
Soundtrack

6/9/58 - 3
Johnny's Greatest Hits...
Johnny Mathis

7/21/58 - 10
Gigi...*Soundtrack*

8/11/58 - 7
Tchaikovsky: Piano Concerto
No. 1...*Van Cliburn*

10/6/58 - 8
Sing Along With Mitch...
Mitch Miller & The Gang

10/13/58 - 5
Frank Sinatra sings for Only The
Lonely...*Frank Sinatra*

11/24/58 - 1
The Kingston Trio...
The Kingston Trio

12/29/58 - 2
Christmas Sing-Along With Mitch...
Mitch Miller & The Gang

2/2/59 - 3
Flower Drum Song...
Original Cast

2/23/59 - 10
The Music From Peter Gunn...
Henry Mancini

6/22/59 - 5
Exotica...*Martin Denny*

7/13/59 - 1
Film Encores...
Mantovani

7/27/59 - 15
The Kingston Trio At Large...
The Kingston Trio

11/9/59 - 5
Heavenly...*Johnny Mathis*

12/14/59 - 8
Here We Go Again!...
The Kingston Trio

1/11/60 - 1
The Lord's Prayer...
The Mormon Tabernacle Choir

1/25/60 - 16
The Sound Of Music...
Original Cast

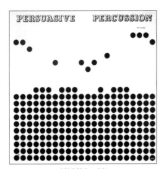

4/25/60 - 13
Persuasive Percussion...
Terry Snyder and The All-Stars

5/2/60 - 2
Theme from A Summer Place...
Billy Vaughn

5/9/60 - 12
Sold Out...*The Kingston Trio*

7/25/60 - 14
**The Button-Down Mind Of Bob
Newhart**...*Bob Newhart*

8/29/60 - 10
String Along...
The Kingston Trio

10/24/60 - 9
Nice 'n' Easy...*Frank Sinatra*

12/5/60 - 10
G.I. Blues...
Elvis Presley/Soundtrack

1/9/61 - 1
The Button-Down Mind Strikes Back!...*Bob Newhart*

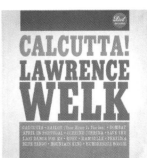

1/16/61 - 5
Wonderland By Night...
Bert Kaempfert

1/23/61 - 14
Exodus...*Soundtrack*

3/13/61 - 11
Calcutta!...*Lawrence Welk*

6/5/61 - 6
Camelot...*Original Cast*

7/17/61 - 9
Stars For A Summer Night...
Various Artists

7/17/61 - 1
Carnival...*Original Cast*

8/21/61 - 3
Something for Everybody...
Elvis Presley

9/11/61 - 13
Judy At Carnegie Hall...
Judy Garland

11/20/61 - 7
Stereo 35/MM...
Enoch Light & The Light Brigade

1961 / 1962 / 1963

12/11/61 - 20
Blue Hawaii...
Elvis Presley/Soundtrack

1/6/62 - 1
Holiday Sing Along With Mitch...
Mitch Miller And The Gang

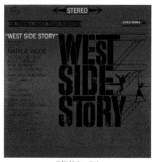

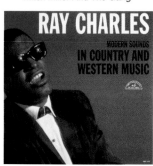

2/10/62 - 12
Breakfast At Tiffany's...
Henry Mancini/Soundtrack

5/5/62 - 54
West Side Story...
Soundtrack

6/23/62 - 14
Modern Sounds In Country And Western Music... *Ray Charles*

10/20/62 - 7
Peter, Paul and Mary...
Peter, Paul & Mary

12/1/62 - 2
My Son, The Folk Singer...
Allan Sherman

12/15/62 - 12
The First Family...
Vaughn Meader

3/9/63 - 1
My Son, The Celebrity...
Allan Sherman

3/9/63 - 1
Jazz Samba...
Stan Getz/Charlie Byrd

3/16/63 - 5
**Songs I Sing On The Jackie
Gleason Show**...*Frank Fontaine*

5/4/63 - 16
Days of Wine and Roses...
Andy Williams

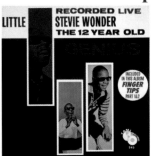

8/24/63 - 1
**Little Stevie Wonder/The 12 Year
Old Genius**...*Stevie Wonder*

8/31/63 - 8
My Son, The Nut...
Allan Sherman

11/2/63 - 5
In The Wind...
Peter, Paul & Mary

12/7/63 - 10
The Singing Nun...
The Singing Nun

2/15/64 - 11
Meet The Beatles!...
The Beatles

5/2/64 - 5
The Beatles' Second Album...
The Beatles

6/6/64 - 1
Hello, Dolly!...*Original Cast*

6/13/64 - 6
Hello, Dolly!...
Louis Armstrong

7/25/64 - 14
A Hard Day's Night...
The Beatles/Soundtrack

1964 / 1965

10/31/64 - 5
People...*Barbra Streisand*

12/5/64 - 4
Beach Boys Concert...
The Beach Boys

1/2/65 - 1
Roustabout...
Elvis Presley/Soundtrack

1/9/65 - 9
Beatles '65...*The Beatles*

3/13/65 - 14
Mary Poppins...
Soundtrack

3/20/65 - 3
Goldfinger...*Soundtrack*

7/10/65 - 6
Beatles VI...*The Beatles*

8/21/65 - 3
Out Of Our Heads...
The Rolling Stones

9/11/65 - 9
Help!...
The Beatles/Soundtrack

11/13/65 - 2
The Sound Of Music...
Soundtrack

11/27/65 - 8
Whipped Cream & Other Delights...
Herb Alpert's Tijuana Brass

1/8/66 - 6
Rubber Soul...*The Beatles*

3/5/66 - 6
Going Places...
Herb Alpert and the Tijuana Brass

3/12/66 - 5
Ballads of the Green Berets...
SSgt Barry Sadler

5/21/66 - 1
**If You Can Believe Your Eyes And
Ears**...*The Mama's & The Papa's*

5/28/66 - 9
What Now My Love...
Herb Alpert & The Tijuana Brass

7/23/66 - 1
Strangers In The Night...
Frank Sinatra

7/30/66 - 5
"Yesterday"...And Today...
The Beatles

9/10/66 - 6
Revolver...*The Beatles*

10/22/66 - 2
The Supremes A' Go-Go...
The Supremes

11/5/66 - 1
Doctor Zhivago...
Soundtrack

11/12/66 - 13
The Monkees...*The Monkees*

1967 / 1968

2/11/67 - 18
More Of The Monkees...
The Monkees

6/17/67 - 1
...Sounds Like...
Herb Alpert & The Tijuana Brass

6/24/67 - 1
Headquarters...*The Monkees*

7/1/67 - 15
Sgt. Pepper's Lonely Hearts Club Band...*The Beatles*

10/14/67 - 2
Ode To Billie Joe...
Bobbie Gentry

10/28/67 - 5
Diana Ross and the Supremes Greatest Hits...*The Supremes*

12/2/67 - 5
Pisces, Aquarius, Capricorn & Jones Ltd....*The Monkees*

1/6/68 - 8
Magical Mystery Tour...
The Beatles/Soundtrack

3/2/68 - 5
Blooming Hits...*Paul Mauriat*

4/6/68 - 9
The Graduate...
Simon & GarfunkelSoundtrack

5/25/68 - 7
Bookends...*Simon & Garfunkel*

7/27/68 - 2
The Beat Of The Brass...
Herb Alpert & The Tijuana Brass

8/10/68 - 4
Wheels Of Fire...*Cream*

9/7/68 - 4
Waiting For The Sun...
The Doors

9/28/68 - 1
**Time Peace/The Rascals' Greatest
Hits**...*The Rascals*

10/12/68 - 8
Cheap Thrills...
Big Brother & The Holding Company

11/16/68 - 2
Electric Ladyland...
Jimi Hendrix Experience

12/21/68 - 5
Wichita Lineman...
Glen Campbell

12/28/68 - 9
The Beatles [White Album]...
The Beatles

2/8/69 - 1
TCB...*Diana Ross & The Supremes
with The Temptations*

3/29/69 - 7
Blood, Sweat & Tears...
Blood, Sweat & Tears

1969 / 1970

4/26/69 - 13
Hair...*Original Cast*

8/23/69 - 4
Johnny Cash At San Quentin...
Johnny Cash

9/20/69 - 2
Blind Faith...*Blind Faith*

10/4/69 - 4
Green River...
Creedence Clearwater Revival

11/1/69 - 11
Abbey Road...*The Beatles*

12/27/69 - 7
Led Zeppelin II...*Led Zeppelin*

1970

3/7/70 - 10
Bridge Over Troubled Water...
Simon & Garfunkel

5/16/70 - 1
Deja Vu...
Crosby, Stills, Nash & Young

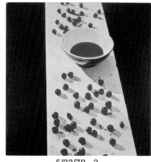

5/23/70 - 3
McCartney...*Paul McCartney*

6/13/70 - 4
Let It Be...*The Beatles*

7/11/70 - 4
Woodstock...*Soundtrack*

8/8/70 - 2
Blood, Sweat & Tears 3...
Blood, Sweat & Tears

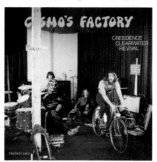

8/22/70 - 9
Cosmo's Factory...
Creedence Clearwater Revival

10/24/70 - 6
Abraxas...*Santana*

10/31/70 - 4
Led Zeppelin III...
Led Zeppelin

1971

1/2/71 - 7
All Things Must Pass...
George Harrison

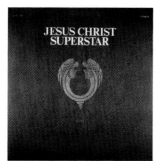

2/20/71 - 3
Jesus Christ Superstar...
Various Artists

2/27/71 - 9
Pearl...*Janis Joplin*

5/15/71 - 1
4 Way Street...
Crosby, Stills, Nash & Young

5/22/71 - 4
Sticky Fingers...
The Rolling Stones

6/19/71 - 15
Tapestry...*Carole King*

10/2/71 - 4
Every Picture Tells A Story...
Rod Stewart

1971 / 1972

10/30/71 - 1
Imagine...*John Lennon*

11/6/71 - 1
Shaft...
Isaac Hayes/Soundtrack

11/13/71 - 5
Santana III...*Santana*

12/18/71 - 2
There's A Riot Goin' On...
Sly & The Family Stone

1972

1/1/72 - 3
Music...*Carole King*

1/22/72 - 7
American Pie...*Don McLean*

3/11/72 - 2
Harvest...*Neil Young*

3/25/72 - 5
America...*America*

4/29/72 - 5
First Take...*Roberta Flack*

6/3/72 - 2
Thick As A Brick...*Jethro Tull*

6/17/72 - 4
Exile On Main St....
The Rolling Stones

7/15/72 - 5
Honky Chateau...*Elton John*

8/19/72 - 9
Chicago V...*Chicago*

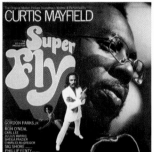

10/21/72 - 4
Superfly...
Curtis Mayfield/Soundtrack

11/18/72 - 3
Catch Bull At Four...
Cat Stevens

12/9/72 - 5
Seventh Sojourn...
The Moody Blues

1973

1/13/73 - 5
No Secrets...*Carly Simon*

2/17/73 - 2
The World Is A Ghetto...*War*

3/3/73 - 2
**Don't Shoot Me I'm Only The Piano
Player**...*Elton John*

3/17/73 - 3
Dueling Banjos...
"Deliverance" Soundtrack

4/7/73 - 2
Lady Sings The Blues...
Diana Ross/Soundtrack

4/21/73 - 1
Billion Dollar Babies...
Alice Cooper

1973

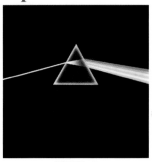

4/28/73 - 1
The Dark Side Of The Moon...
Pink Floyd

5/5/73 - 1
Aloha from Hawaii via Satellite...
Elvis Presley

5/12/73 - 2
Houses Of The Holy...
Led Zeppelin

5/26/73 - 1
The Beatles/1967-1970...
The Beatles

6/2/73 - 3
Red Rose Speedway...
Paul McCartney & Wings

6/23/73 - 5
Living In The Material World...
George Harrison

7/28/73 - 5
Chicago VI...*Chicago*

8/18/73 - 1
A Passion Play...*Jethro Tull*

9/8/73 - 5
Brothers And Sisters...
The Allman Brothers Band

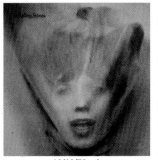

10/13/73 - 4
Goats Head Soup...
The Rolling Stones

11/10/73 - 8
Goodbye Yellow Brick Road...
Elton John

1974

1/5/74 - 1
The Singles 1969-1973...
Carpenters

1/12/74 - 5
You Don't Mess Around With Jim...
Jim Croce

2/16/74 - 4
Planet Waves...*Bob Dylan*

3/16/74 - 2
The Way We Were...
Barbra Streisand

3/30/74 - 3
John Denver's Greatest Hits...
John Denver

4/13/74 - 4
Band On The Run...
Paul McCartney & Wings

4/27/74 - 1
Chicago VII...*Chicago*

5/4/74 - 5
The Sting...
Marvin Hamlisch/Soundtrack

6/22/74 - 2
Sundown...*Gordon Lightfoot*

7/13/74 - 4
Caribou...*Elton John*

8/10/74 - 1
Back Home Again...*John Denver*

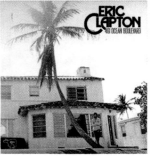

8/17/74 - 4
461 Ocean Boulevard...
Eric Clapton

1974

9/14/74 - 2
Fulfillingness' First Finale...
Stevie Wonder

9/28/74 - 1
Bad Company...*Bad Company*

10/5/74 - 1
Endless Summer...
The Beach Boys

10/12/74 - 1
If You Love Me, Let Me Know...
Olivia Newton-John

10/19/74 - 1
Not Fragile...
Bachman-Turner Overdrive

10/26/74 - 1
Can't Get Enough...*Barry White*

11/2/74 - 1
So Far...
Crosby, Stills, Nash & Young

11/9/74 - 1
Wrap Around Joy...*Carole King*

11/16/74 - 1
Walls And Bridges...
John Lennon

1975

11/23/74 - 1
It's Only Rock 'N Roll...
The Rolling Stones

11/30/74 - 10
Elton John - Greatest Hits...
Elton John

2/8/75 - 1
Fire...*Ohio Players*

2/15/75 - 1
Heart Like A Wheel...
Linda Ronstadt

2/22/75 - 1
AWB...*Average White Band*

3/1/75 - 2
Blood On The Tracks...
Bob Dylan

3/15/75 - 1
Have You Never Been Mellow...
Olivia Newton-John

3/22/75 - 6
Physical Graffiti...
Led Zeppelin

5/3/75 - 2
Chicago VIII...*Chicago*

5/17/75 - 3
That's The Way Of The World...
Earth, Wind & Fire/Soundtrack

6/7/75 - 7
**Captain Fantastic And The Brown
Dirt Cowboy**...*Elton John*

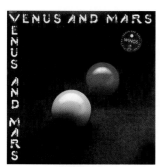

7/19/75 - 1
Venus And Mars...*Wings*

7/26/75 - 5
One Of These Nights...*Eagles*

9/6/75 - 4
Red Octopus...
Jefferson Starship

1975 / 1976

9/13/75 - 1
The Heat Is On...
The Isley Brothers

9/20/75 - 1
Between The Lines...*Janis Ian*

10/4/75 - 2
Wish You Were Here...
Pink Floyd

10/18/75 - 2
Windsong...*John Denver*

11/8/75 - 3
Rock Of The Westies...
Elton John

12/6/75 - 1
Still Crazy After All These Years...
Paul Simon

12/13/75 - 5
Chicago IX - Chicago's Greatest Hits...*Chicago*

1976

1/17/76 - 3
Gratitude...*Earth, Wind & Fire*

2/7/76 - 5
Desire...*Bob Dylan*

3/13/76 - 5
Eagles/Their Greatest Hits
1971-1975...*Eagles*

4/10/76 - 10
Frampton Comes Alive!...
Peter Frampton

4/24/76 - 7
Wings At The Speed Of Sound...
Wings

5/1/76 - 2
Presence*...Led Zeppelin*

5/15/76 - 4
Black And Blue...
The Rolling Stones

7/31/76 - 2
Breezin'*...George Benson*

9/4/76 - 1
Fleetwood Mac*...Fleetwood Mac*

10/16/76 - 14
Songs In The Key Of Life...
Stevie Wonder

1/15/77 - 8
Hotel California*...Eagles*

1/22/77 - 1
Wings Over America*...Wings*

2/12/77 - 6
A Star Is Born...
Barbra Streisand/Soundtrack

4/2/77 - 31
Rumours*...Fleetwood Mac*

7/16/77 - 1
Barry Manilow/Live...
Barry Manilow

12/3/77 - 5
Simple Dreams...*Linda Ronstadt*

1/21/78 - 24
Saturday Night Fever...
Bee Gees/Soundtrack

7/8/78 - 1
City to City...*Gerry Rafferty*

7/15/78 - 2
Some Girls...
The Rolling Stones

7/29/78 - 12
Grease...*Soundtrack*

9/16/78 - 2
Don't Look Back...*Boston*

11/4/78 - 1
Living In The USA...
Linda Ronstadt

11/11/78 - 1
Live And More...*Donna Summer*

11/18/78 - 8
52nd Street...*Billy Joel*

1/6/79 - 3 — **Barbra Streisand's
Greatest Hits, Volume 2**...
Barbra Streisand

2/3/79 - 1
Briefcase Full Of Blues...
Blues Brothers

2/10/79 - 3
Blondes Have More Fun...
Rod Stewart

3/3/79 - 6
Spirits Having Flown...
Bee Gees

4/7/79 - 5
Minute By Minute...
The Doobie Brothers

5/19/79 - 6
Breakfast In America...
Supertramp

6/16/79 - 6
Bad Girls...*Donna Summer*

8/11/79 - 5
Get The Knack...*The Knack*

9/15/79 - 7
In Through The Out Door...
Led Zeppelin

11/3/79 - 9
The Long Run...*Eagles*

1/5/80 - 1
On The Radio-Greatest
Hits-Volumes I & II...*Donna Summer*

1/12/80 - 1
Bee Gees Greatest...*Bee Gees*

1980 / 1981

1/19/80 - 15
The Wall...*Pink Floyd*

5/3/80 - 6
Against The Wind...
Bob Seger & The Silver Bullet Band

6/14/80 - 6
Glass Houses...*Billy Joel*

7/26/80 - 7
Emotional Rescue...
The Rolling Stones

9/13/80 - 1
Hold Out...*Jackson Browne*

9/20/80 - 5
The Game...*Queen*

10/25/80 - 3
Guilty...*Barbra Streisand*

11/8/80 - 4
The River...*Bruce Springsteen*

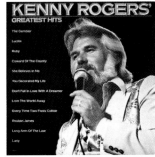

12/13/80 - 2
Kenny Rogers' Greatest Hits...
Kenny Rogers

12/27/80 - 8
Double Fantasy...
John Lennon Yoko Ono

2/21/81 - 15
Hi Infidelity...*REO Speedwagon*

4/4/81 - 3
Paradise Theater...*Styx*

6/27/81 - 4
Mistaken Identity...*Kim Carnes*

7/25/81 - 3
Long Distance Voyager...
The Moody Blues

8/15/81 - 1
Precious Time...*Pat Benatar*

8/22/81 - 10
4...*Foreigner*

9/5/81 - 1
Bella Donna...*Stevie Nicks*

9/12/81 - 1
Escape...*Journey*

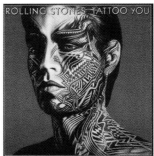

9/19/81 - 9
Tattoo You...
Rolling Stones

12/26/81 - 3
**For Those About To Rock
We Salute You**...*AC/DC*

2/6/82 - 4
Freeze-Frame...
The J. Geils Band

3/6/82 - 6
Beauty And The Beat...*Go-Go's*

1982 / 1983

4/17/82 - 4
Chariots Of Fire...
Vangelis/Soundtrack

5/15/82 - 9
Asia...*Asia*

5/29/82 - 3
Tug Of War...*Paul McCartney*

8/7/82 - 5
Mirage...*Fleetwood Mac*

9/11/82 - 9
American Fool...*John Cougar*

11/13/82 - 15
Business As Usual...
Men At Work

1983

2/26/83 - 37
Thriller...*Michael Jackson*

6/25/83 - 2
Flashdance...*Soundtrack*

7/23/83 - 17
Synchronicity...*The Police*

11/26/83 - 1
Metal Health...*Quiet Riot*

12/3/83 - 3
Can't Slow Down...
Lionel Richie

4/21/84 - 10
Footloose...*Soundtrack*

6/30/84 - 1
Sports...*Huey Lewis & The News*

7/7/84 - 7
Born In The U.S.A.....
Bruce Springsteen

8/4/84 - 24
Purple Rain...
Prince and the Revolution/Soundtrack

2/9/85 - 3
Like A Virgin...*Madonna*

3/2/85 - 3
Make It Big...*Wham!*

3/23/85 - 1
Centerfield...*John Fogerty*

3/30/85 - 7
No Jacket Required...
Phil Collins

4/27/85 - 3
We Are The World...
USA For Africa

6/1/85 - 3
Around The World In A Day...
Prince & The Revolution

39

1985 / 1986

6/22/85 - 2
Beverly Hills Cop...
Soundtrack

7/13/85 - 5
Songs From The Big Chair...
Tears For Fears

8/10/85 - 2
Reckless...*Bryan Adams*

8/31/85 - 9
Brothers In Arms...
Dire Straits

11/2/85 - 11
Miami Vice...*TV Soundtrack*

12/21/85 - 1
Heart...*Heart*

1986

1/25/86 - 3
The Broadway Album...
Barbra Streisand

2/15/86 - 2
Promise...*Sade*

3/1/86 - 1
Welcome To The Real World...
Mr. Mister

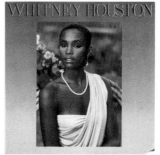

3/8/86 - 14
Whitney Houston...
Whitney Houston

4/26/86 - 3
5150...*Van Halen*

7/5/86 - 2
Control...*Janet Jackson*

7/19/86 - 1
Winner In You...*Patti LaBelle*

7/26/86 - 5
Top Gun...*Soundtrack*

8/16/86 - 5
True Blue...*Madonna*

9/27/86 - 2
Dancing On The Ceiling...
Lionel Richie

10/18/86 - 1
Fore!...*Huey Lewis & The News*

10/25/86 - 8
Slippery When Wet...*Bon Jovi*

11/1/86 - 4
Third Stage...*Boston*

11/29/86 - 7 — Bruce Springsteen
& The E Street Band Live/
1975-85...*Bruce Springsteen*

3/7/87 - 7
Licensed To III...*Beastie Boys*

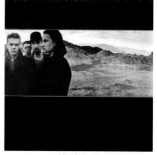

4/25/87 - 9
The Joshua Tree...*U2*

1987 / 1988

6/27/87 - 11
Whitney...*Whitney Houston*

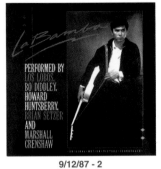

9/12/87 - 2
La Bamba...
Los Lobos/Soundtrack

9/26/87 - 6
Bad...*Michael Jackson*

11/7/87 - 1
Tunnel of Love...
Bruce Springsteen

11/14/87 - 18
Dirty Dancing...*Soundtrack*

1/16/88 - 12
Faith...*George Michael*

1/23/88 - 2
Tiffany...*Tiffany*

6/25/88 - 4
OU812...*Van Halen*

7/23/88 - 6
Hysteria...*Def Leppard*

8/6/88 - 5
Appetite For Destruction...
Guns N' Roses

8/20/88 - 1
Roll With It...*Steve Winwood*

8/27/88 - 1
Tracy Chapman...*Tracy Chapman*

10/15/88 - 4
New Jersey...*Bon Jovi*

11/12/88 - 6
Rattle And Hum...
U2/Soundtrack

12/24/88 - 4
Giving You The Best That I Got...
Anita Baker

1989

1/21/89 - 6
Don't Be Cruel...*Bobby Brown*

3/11/89 - 5
Electric Youth...*Debbie Gibson*

4/15/89 - 1
Loc-ed After Dark...*Tone Loc*

4/22/89 - 6
Like A Prayer...*Madonna*

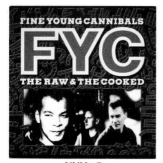

6/3/89 - 7
The Raw & The Cooked...
Fine Young Cannibals

7/22/89 - 6
Batman...
Prince/Soundtrack

9/2/89 - 1
Repeat Offender...*Richard Marx*

1989 / 1990

9/9/89 - 2
Hangin' Tough...
New Kids On The Block

9/23/89 - 8
Girl You Know It's True...
Milli Vanilli

10/7/89 - 10
Forever Your Girl...
Paula Abdul

10/14/89 - 2
Dr. Feelgood...*Mötley Crüe*

10/28/89 - 4
Janet Jackson's Rhythm Nation 1814...*Janet Jackson*

12/16/89 - 1
Storm Front...*Billy Joel*

1990

1/6/90 - 3
...But Seriously...*Phil Collins*

4/7/90 - 3
Nick Of Time...*Bonnie Raitt*

4/28/90 - 6
I Do Not Want What I Haven't Got...
Sinéad O'Connor

6/9/90 - 21
Please Hammer Don't Hurt 'Em...
M.C. Hammer

6/30/90 - 1
Step By Step...
New Kids On The Block

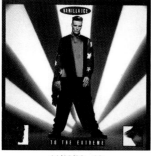

11/10/90 - 16
To The Extreme...*Vanilla Ice*

3/2/91 - 11
Mariah Carey...*Mariah Carey*

5/18/91 - 2
Out Of Time...*R.E.M.*

5/25/91 - 1
Time, Love & Tenderness...
Michael Bolton

6/8/91 - 2
Spellbound...*Paula Abdul*

6/22/91 - 1
EFIL4ZAGGIN...*N.W.A.*

6/29/91 - 1
Slave To The Grind...*Skid Row*

7/6/91 - 3
For Unlawful Carnal Knowledge...
Van Halen

7/27/91 - 5
Unforgettable With Love...
Natalie Cole

8/31/91 - 4
Metallica...*Metallica*

9/28/91 - 18
Ropin' The Wind...*Garth Brooks*

1991 / 1992

10/5/91 - 2
Use Your Illusion II...
Guns N' Roses

12/7/91 - 1
Achtung Baby...*U2*

12/14/91 - 4
Dangerous...*Michael Jackson*

1/11/92 - 2
Nevermind...*Nirvana*

4/4/92 - 2
Wayne's World...
Soundtrack

4/18/92 - 5
Adrenalize...*Def Leppard*

5/23/92 - 2
Totally Krossed Out...
Kris Kross

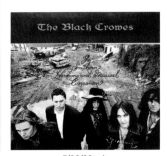

5/30/92 - 1
**The Southern Harmony And Musical
Companion**...*The Black Crowes*

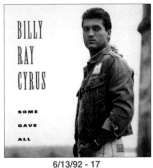

6/13/92 - 17
Some Gave All...
Billy Ray Cyrus

10/10/92 - 7
The Chase...*Garth Brooks*

11/21/92 - 1
Timeless (The Classics)...
Michael Bolton

1993

12/5/92 - 1
The Predator...*Ice Cube*

12/12/92 - 20
The Bodyguard...
Whitney Houston/Soundtrack

3/13/93 - 3
Unplugged...*Eric Clapton*

4/10/93 - 1
Songs Of Faith And Devotion...
Depeche Mode

5/8/93 - 1
Get A Grip...*Aerosmith*

6/5/93 - 6
janet....*Janet Jackson*

7/17/93 - 1
Back To Broadway...
Barbra Streisand

7/24/93 - 2
Zooropa...*U2*

8/7/93 - 2
Black Sunday...*Cypress Hill*

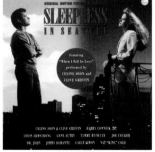

8/21/93 - 1
Sleepless In Seattle...
Soundtrack

8/28/93 - 3
River Of Dreams...*Billy Joel*

1993 / 1994

9/18/93 - 5
In Pieces...*Garth Brooks*

10/9/93 - 1
In Utero...*Nirvana*

10/30/93 - 1
Bat Out Of Hell II: Back Into Hell...
Meat Loaf

11/6/93 - 5
Vs....*Pearl Jam*

12/11/93 - 3
Doggy Style...*Snoop Doggy Dogg*

12/25/93 - 8
Music Box...*Mariah Carey*

1994

2/12/94 - 1
Jar Of Flies...*Alice In Chains*

2/19/94 - 1
Kickin' It Up...
John Michael Montgomery

2/26/94 - 2
Toni Braxton...*Toni Braxton*

3/26/94 - 1
Superunknown...*Soundgarden*

4/2/94 - 2
The Sign...*Ace Of Base*

4/9/94 - 1
Far Beyond Driven...*Pantera*

4/16/94 - 1
Longing In Their Hearts...
Bonnie Raitt

4/23/94 - 4
The Division Bell...*Pink Floyd*

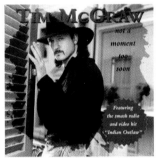

5/21/94 - 2
Not A Moment Too Soon...
Tim McGraw

6/4/94 - 1
The Crow...*Soundtrack*

6/18/94 - 1
III Communication...
Beastie Boys

6/25/94 - 3
Purple...*Stone Temple Pilots*

7/16/94 - 10
The Lion King...
Soundtrack

9/17/94 - 5
II...*Boyz II Men*

10/1/94 - 1
From The Cradle...*Eric Clapton*

10/15/94 - 2
Monster...*R.E.M.*

11/5/94 - 2
Murder Was The Case...
Soundtrack

11/19/94 - 1
MTV Unplugged In New York...
Nirvana

11/26/94 - 2
Hell Freezes Over...*Eagles*

12/10/94 - 3
Miracles - The Holiday Album...
Kenny G

12/24/94 - 1
Vitalogy...*Pearl Jam*

1/7/95 - 8
The Hits...*Garth Brooks*

2/11/95 - 1
Balance...*Van Halen*

3/18/95 - 2
Greatest Hits...
Bruce Springsteen

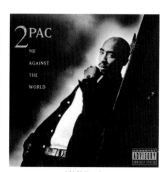

4/1/95 - 4
Me Against The World...*2 Pac*

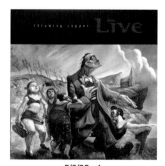

5/6/95 - 1
Throwing Copper...*Live*

5/13/95 - 2
Friday...*Soundtrack*

5/27/95 - 8
Cracked Rear View...
Hootie & The Blowfish

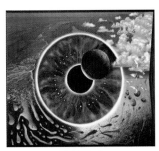

6/24/95 - 1
Pulse...*Pink Floyd*

7/8/95 - 2
HIStory: Past, Present And Future -
Book I...*Michael Jackson*

7/22/95 - 1
Pocahontas...*Soundtrack*

8/5/95 - 1
Dreaming Of You...*Selena*

8/12/95 - 2
E. 1999 Eternal...
Bone thugs-n-harmony

9/2/95 - 4
Dangerous Minds...
Soundtrack

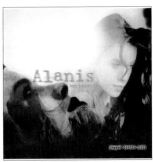

10/7/95 - 12
Jagged Little Pill...
Alanis Morissette

10/21/95 - 6
Daydream...*Mariah Carey*

11/11/95 - 1
Mellon Collie And The Infinite
Sadness...*Smashing Pumpkins*

11/18/95 - 1
Dogg Food...*Tha Dogg Pound*

11/25/95 - 1
Alice In Chains...
Alice In Chains

12/2/95 - 1
R. Kelly...*R. Kelly*

Pop   1995 / 1996

12/9/95 - 3
Anthology 1...*The Beatles*

1/20/96 - 5
Waiting To Exhale...
Soundtrack

3/2/96 - 2
All Eyez On Me...*2Pac*

4/6/96 - 1
Anthology 2...*The Beatles*

5/4/96 - 1
Evil Empire...
Rage Against The Machine

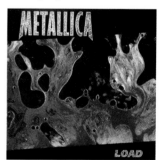

5/11/96 - 2
Fairweather Johnson...
Hootie & The Blowfish

5/25/96 - 4
The Score...*Fugees*

6/22/96 - 4
Load...*Metallica*

7/20/96 - 4
It Was Written...*Nas*

8/17/96 - 1
Beats, Rhymes And Life...
A Tribe Called Quest

9/14/96 - 2
No Code...*Pearl Jam*

9/28/96 - 1
Home Again...*New Edition*

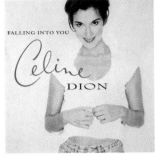

10/5/96 - 3
Falling Into You...*Celine Dion*

10/19/96 - 1
From The Muddy Banks Of The Wishkah...*Nirvana*

11/2/96 - 1
Recovering The Satellites...
Counting Crows

11/9/96 - 1
Best Of Volume 1...*Van Halen*

11/16/96 - 1
Anthology 3...*The Beatles*

11/23/96 - 1
The Don Killuminati - The 7 Day Theory...*Makaveli*

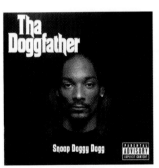

11/30/96 - 1
Tha Doggfather...
Snoop Doggy Dogg

12/7/96 - 2
Razorblade Suitcase...*Bush*

12/21/96 - 9
Tragic Kingdom...*No Doubt*

1997

2/15/97 - 1
Gridlock'd...*Soundtrack*

1997

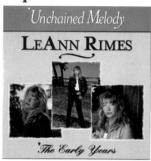

3/1/97 - 1
Unchained Melody/The Early Years...*LeAnn Rimes*

3/8/97 - 1
Secret Samadhi...*Live*

3/15/97 - 1
Private Parts...
Soundtrack

3/22/97 - 1
Pop...*U2*

3/29/97 - 1
The Untouchable...*Scarface*

4/5/97 - 1
Nine Lives...*Aerosmith*

4/12/97 - 4
Life After Death...
The Notorious B.I.G.

5/10/97 - 1
Share My World...*Mary J. Blige*

5/17/97 - 1
Carrying Your Love With Me...
George Strait

5/24/97 - 5
Spice...*Spice Girls*

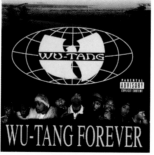

6/21/97 - 1
Wu-Tang Forever...*Wu-Tang Clan*

6/28/97 - 2 — Butterfly Kisses (Shades Of Grace)...
Bob Carlisle

7/19/97 - 1
The Fat Of The Land...*Prodigy*

7/26/97 - 2
Men In Black - The Album...
Soundtrack

8/9/97 - 4
No Way Out...
Puff Daddy & The Family

8/16/97 - 1
The Art Of War...
Bone thugs-n-harmony

9/6/97 - 1
The Dance...*Fleetwood Mac*

9/20/97 - 1
Ghetto D...*Master P*

9/27/97 - 3
You Light Up My Life - Inspirational Songs...*LeAnn Rimes*

10/4/97 - 1
Butterfly...*Mariah Carey*

10/11/97 - 1
Evolution...*Boyz II Men*

10/25/97 - 1
The Velvet Rope...*Janet Jackson*

11/8/97 - 1
The Firm - The Album...
The Firm

11/15/97 - 2
Harlem World...*Mase*

Pop
1997 / 1998

11/29/97 - 1
Higher Ground...
Barbra Streisand

12/6/97 - 1
Reload...*Metallica*

12/13/97 - 5
Sevens...*Garth Brooks*

1/17/98 - 1
Let's Talk About Love...
Celine Dion

1/24/98 - 16
Titanic...*Soundtrack*

5/16/98 - 1
Before These Crowded Streets...
Dave Matthews Band

5/23/98 - 2
The Limited Series (boxed set)...
Garth Brooks

6/6/98 - 1
It's Dark And Hell Is Hot...
DMX

6/13/98 - 3
City Of Angels...
Soundtrack

6/20/98 - 2
MP Da Last Don...*Master P*

7/18/98 - 2
Armageddon...*Soundtrack*

8/1/98 - 3
Hello Nasty...*Beastie Boys*

8/22/98 - 2
Da Game Is To Be Sold, Not To Be Told...*Snoop Dogg*

9/5/98 - 1
Follow The Leader...*Korn*

9/12/98 - 4
The Miseducation Of Lauryn Hill...
Lauryn Hill

10/3/98 - 1
Mechanical Animals...
Marilyn Manson

10/17/98 - 5
Vol. 2...Hard Knock Life...
Jay-Z

11/21/98 - 2
Supposed Former Infatuation Junkie...*Alanis Morissette*

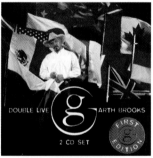

12/5/98 - 5
Double Live...*Garth Brooks*

1/9/99 - 3
Flesh Of My Flesh Blood Of My Blood...*DMX*

1/30/99 - 6
...Baby One More Time...
Britney Spears

2/6/99 - 1
Made Man...*Silkk The Shocker*

2/13/99 - 1
Chyna Doll...*Foxy Brown*

3/13/99 - 5
Fanmail...*TLC*

4/24/99 - 2
I Am......*Nas*

5/15/99 - 1
Ruff Ryders - Ryde Or Die Vol. I...
Ruff Ryders

5/22/99 - 1
A Place In The Sun...
Tim McGraw

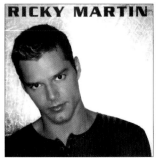

5/29/99 - 1
Ricky Martin...*Ricky Martin*

6/5/99 - 10
Millennium...*Backstreet Boys*

7/10/99 - 4
Significant Other...
Limp Bizkit

9/11/99 - 1
Christina Aguilera...
Christina Aguilera

9/18/99 - 2
Fly...*Dixie Chicks*

10/2/99 - 1
Ruff Ryders' First Lady...*Eve*

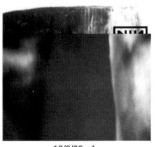

10/9/99 - 1
The Fragile...*Nine Inch Nails*

1999 / 2000 Pop

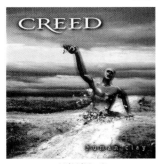

10/16/99 - 2
Human Clay...*Creed*

10/30/99 - 12
Supernatural...*Santana*

11/20/99 - 1
The Battle Of Los Angeles...
Rage Against The Machine

11/27/99 - 1
Breathe...*Faith Hill*

12/4/99 - 1
Issues...*Korn*

12/11/99 - 3
All The Way...A Decade Of Song...
Celine Dion

12/25/99 - 1
Born Again...
The Notorious B.I.G.

2000

1/8/00 - 1
...And Then There Was X...*DMX*

1/15/00 - 1
**Vol. 3...Life And Times Of S.
Carter**...*Jay-Z*

2/12/00 - 2
Voodoo...*D'Angelo*

4/8/00 - 8
No Strings Attached...**NSYNC*

6/3/00 - 1
Oops!...I Did It Again...
Britney Spears

6/10/00 - 8
The Marshall Mathers LP...
Eminem

8/5/00 - 3
Now 4...*Various Artists*

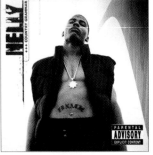

8/26/00 - 5
Country Grammar...*Nelly*

9/30/00 - 1 — **G.O.A.T. Featuring
James T. Smith The Greatest Of All
Time**...*LL Cool J*

10/7/00 - 1
Music...*Madonna*

10/14/00 - 1
Let's Get Ready...*Mystikal*

10/21/00 - 1
Kid A...*Radiohead*

10/28/00 - 1
Rule 3:36...*Ja Rule*

11/4/00 - 2
**Chocolate Starfish And The Hot Dog
Flavored Water**...*Limp Bizkit*

11/18/00 - 1
**The Dynasty Roc La Familia
(2000 -)**...*Jay-Z*

11/25/00 - 1
TP-2.com...*R. Kelly*

2000 / 2001   Pop

12/2/00 - 8
1...*The Beatles*

12/9/00 - 2
Black & Blue...*Backstreet Boys*

2/10/01 - 1
J.Lo...*Jennifer Lopez*

2/17/01 - 6
Hotshot...*Shaggy*

3/17/01 - 2
Everyday...*Dave Matthews Band*

4/14/01 - 1
Until The End Of Time...*2Pac*

4/21/01 - 3
Now 6...
Various Artists

5/12/01 - 1
All For You...*Janet Jackson*

5/19/01 - 2
Survivor...*Destiny's Child*

6/2/01 - 1
Lateralus...*Tool*

6/9/01 - 3
Break The Cycle...*Staind*

61

6/30/01 - 1
Take Off Your Pants And Jacket...
Blink-182

7/7/01 - 2
Devil's Night...*D12*

7/14/01 - 3
Songs In A Minor...*Alicia Keys*

8/11/01 - 1
Celebrity...**NSYNC*

8/18/01 - 3
Now 7...
Various Artists

9/8/01 - 1
Now...*Maxwell*

9/15/01 - 1
Aaliyah...*Aaliyah*

9/22/01 - 1
Toxicity...*System Of A Down*

9/29/01 - 3
The Blueprint...*Jay-Z*

10/20/01 - 2
Pain Is Love...*Ja Rule*

11/3/01 - 1
God Bless America...
Various Artists

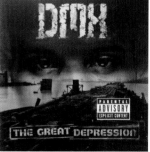

11/10/01 - 1
The Great Depression...*DMX*

11/17/01 - 1
Invincible...*Michael Jackson*

11/24/01 - 1
Britney...*Britney Spears*

12/1/01 - 1
Scarecrow...*Garth Brooks*

12/8/01 - 8
Weathered...*Creed*

2002

2/2/02 - 4
Drive...*Alan Jackson*

2/23/02 - 2
J To Tha L-O! The Remixes...
Jennifer Lopez

3/16/02 - 1
Under Rug Swept...
Alanis Morissette

3/23/02 - 2
O Brother, Where Art Thou?...
Soundtrack

4/6/02 - 1
Now 9...
Various Artists

4/13/02 - 1
A New Day Has Come...
Celine Dion

4/20/02 - 3
Ashanti...*Ashanti*

2002

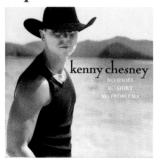

5/11/02 - 1
No Shoes, No Shirt, No Problems...
Kenny Chesney

5/18/02 - 1
Hood Rich...*Big Tymers*

5/25/02 - 1
JUSLISEN (Just Listen)...*Musiq*

6/1/02 - 1 — P. Diddy & Bad Boy
Records Present...We Invented The
Remix...*Various Artists*

6/8/02 - 6
The Eminem Show...*Eminem*

7/13/02 - 4
Nellyville...*Nelly*

8/3/02 - 1
Busted Stuff...
Dave Matthews Band

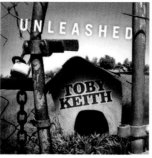

8/10/02 - 1
Unleashed...*Toby Keith*

8/17/02 - 2
The Rising...*Bruce Springsteen*

9/14/02 - 4
Home...*Dixie Chicks*

10/5/02 - 1
Believe...*Disturbed*

10/12/02 - 3
Elv1s: 30 #1 Hits...
Elvis Presley

11/2/02 - 1
Cry...*Faith Hill*

11/9/02 - 1
Shaman...*Santana*

11/16/02 - 4
8 Mile...*Soundtrack*

11/30/02 - 1
The Blueprint 2: The Gift And The Curse...*Jay-Z*

12/7/02 - 5
Up!...*Shania Twain*

1/25/03 - 4
Come Away With Me...
Norah Jones

2/22/03 - 6
Get Rich Or Die Tryin'...
50 Cent

3/8/03 - 1
Chocolate Factory...*R. Kelly*

4/12/03 - 2
Meteora...*Linkin Park*

4/26/03 - 1
Faceless...*Godsmack*

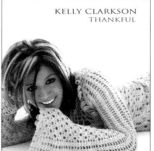

5/3/03 - 1
Thankful...*Kelly Clarkson*

5/10/03 - 1
American Life...*Madonna*

5/24/03 - 1 — **Body Kiss**...
The Isley Brothers Featuring Ronald Isley AKA Mr. Biggs

5/31/03 - 1
The Golden Age Of Grotesque...
Marilyn Manson

6/7/03 - 1
14 Shades Of Grey...*Staind*

6/14/03 - 1
How The West Was Won...
Led Zeppelin

6/21/03 - 1
St. Anger...*Metallica*

6/28/03 - 1
Dance With My Father...
Luther Vandross

7/5/03 - 1
After The Storm...*Monica*

7/12/03 - 1
Dangerously In Love...*Beyoncé*

7/19/03 - 2
Chapter II...*Ashanti*

8/2/03 - 4
Bad Boys II...*Soundtrack*

8/30/03 - 1
Greatest Hits Volume II and Some Other Stuff...*Alan Jackson*

9/6/03 - 1
The Neptunes Present...Clones...
Various Artists

9/13/03 - 1
Love & Life...*Mary J. Blige*

9/20/03 - 1
Metamorphosis...*Hilary Duff*

9/27/03 - 1
Heavier Things...*John Mayer*

10/4/03 - 1
Grand Champ...*DMX*

10/11/03 - 7
Speakerboxxx/The Love Below...
OutKast

10/25/03 - 1
Chicken*N*Beer...*Ludacris*

11/1/03 - 2
Measure Of A Man...*Clay Aiken*

11/22/03 - 1
Shock'n Y'all...*Toby Keith*

11/29/03 - 2
The Black Album...*Jay-Z*

12/6/03 - 1
In The Zone...*Britney Spears*

12/20/03 - 2
The Diary Of Alicia Keys...
Alicia Keys

2003 / 2004

2004

12/27/03 - 1
Soulful...*Ruben Studdard*

1/24/04 - 1
Closer...*Josh Groban*

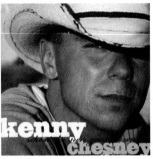

2/14/04 - 1
Kamikaze...*Twista*

2/21/04 - 1
When The Sun Goes Down...
Kenny Chesney

2/28/04 - 3+
Feels Like Home...
Norah Jones

The All-Time #1 Pop Albums

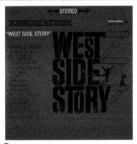

❶ **South Pacific**...*Original Cast*
69 weeks at #1 — Year: 1949

❷ **West Side Story**...*Soundtrack*
54 weeks at #1 — Year: 1962

❸ **The Student Prince and other great musical comedies** ...*Mario Lanza*
42 weeks at #1 — Year: 1954

❹ **Thriller**...*Michael Jackson*
37 weeks at #1 — Year: 1983

❺ **South Pacific**...*Soundtrack*
31 weeks at #1 — Year: 1958

❻ **Rumours**...*Fleetwood Mac*
31 weeks at #1 — Year: 1977

The #1 R&B Albums

1965-2004

This section displays, in chronological order, full-color representations of the 587 albums that hit #1 on *Billboard's* R&B Albums chart from January 30, 1965 through March 13, 2004. *Billboard* did not publish a Best Selling Soul LP's chart from August 26, 1972 to October 7, 1972. The chart is currently named Top R&B/Hip-Hop Albums.

The date an album first hit #1 is listed below each album's picture. The total weeks the album held the #1 position is listed to the right of the date.

Billboard has not published an issue for the last week of the year since 1976. For the years 1976 through 1991, *Billboard* considered the charts listed in the last published issue of the year to be "frozen" and all chart positions remained the same for the unpublished week. This frozen chart data is included in our tabulations. Since 1992, *Billboard* has compiled the Top R&B/Hip-Hop Albums chart for the last week of the year, even though an issue is not published. This chart is only available through *Billboard's* Web site or by mail. Our tabulations include this unpublished chart data.

1965 / 1966

1/30/65 - 1
Where Did Our Love Go...
The Supremes

2/6/65 - 3
Sam Cooke At The Copa...
Sam Cooke

2/27/65 - 4
Shake...*Sam Cooke*

3/27/65 - 2
People Get Ready...
The Impressions

4/10/65 - 18
The Temptations Sing Smokey...
The Temptations

7/3/65 - 3
Four Tops...*Four Tops*

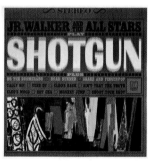

7/24/65 - 1
Shotgun...
Jr. Walker & The All Stars

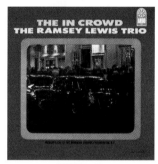

9/11/65 - 12
The In Crowd...
The Ramsey Lewis Trio

10/30/65 - 1
Otis Blue/Otis Redding Sings Soul...
Otis Redding

12/11/65 - 14
Temptin' Temptations...
The Temptations

1/15/66 - 5
Going To A Go-Go...
Smokey Robinson And The Miracles

4/23/66 - 1
I Hear A Symphony...
The Supremes

4/30/66 - 2
Got My Mojo Workin'...
Jimmy Smith

5/14/66 - 1
Crying Time...*Ray Charles*

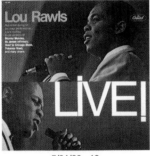

5/21/66 - 12
Lou Rawls Live!...*Lou Rawls*

7/30/66 - 6
Gettin' Ready...
The Temptations

8/20/66 - 1
Hold On, I'm Comin'...
Sam & Dave

10/1/66 - 9
Lou Rawls Soulin'...*Lou Rawls*

10/22/66 - 4
The Supremes A' Go-Go...
The Supremes

12/31/66 - 9
The Temptations Greatest Hits...
The Temptations

2/4/67 - 1
Four Tops Live!...*Four Tops*

3/11/67 - 3 — The Supremes sing
Holland-Dozier-Holland...
The Supremes

1967 / 1968

4/1/67 - 1
Mercy, Mercy, Mercy!...
The Cannonball Adderley Quintet

4/8/67 - 3
Temptations Live!...
The Temptations

4/29/67 - 14
**I Never Loved A Man The Way I
Love You**...*Aretha Franklin*

7/15/67 - 2
Revenge...*Bill Cosby*

7/29/67 - 2
Here Where There is Love...
Dionne Warwick

9/2/67 - 1
With A Lot O' Soul...
The Temptations

9/9/67 - 5
Aretha Arrives...
Aretha Franklin

10/14/67 - 12
**Diana Ross and the Supremes
Greatest Hits**...*The Supremes*

1/6/68 - 7
**The Temptations in a Mellow
Mood**...*The Temptations*

2/24/68 - 1
History Of Otis Redding...
Otis Redding

3/2/68 - 16
Aretha: Lady Soul...
Aretha Franklin

4/20/68 - 3
The Dock Of The Bay...
Otis Redding

6/22/68 - 3
Wish It Would Rain...
The Temptations

7/27/68 - 17
Aretha Now...*Aretha Franklin*

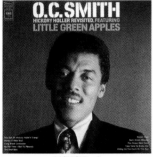

11/23/68 - 1
Hickory Holler Revisited...
O.C. Smith

12/7/68 - 2
Special Occasion...
Smokey Robinson And The Miracles

12/21/68 - 4 — Diana Ross & The
Supremes Join The Temptations...
The Supremes & The Temptations

1/18/69 - 6
TCB...*Diana Ross & The Supremes*
with The Temptations

3/1/69 - 4
Aretha Franklin: Soul '69...
Aretha Franklin

3/29/69 - 13
Cloud Nine...*The Temptations*

6/21/69 - 2
M.P.G....*Marvin Gaye*

7/12/69 - 2
My Whole World Ended...
David Ruffin

7/26/69 - 4
Aretha's Gold...
Aretha Franklin

8/23/69 - 10
Hot Buttered Soul...
Isaac Hayes

11/1/69 - 15
Puzzle People...
The Temptations

1970

2/14/70 - 9
**Diana Ross Presents The
Jackson 5...***Jackson 5*

4/18/70 - 4
Psychedelic Shack...
The Temptations

5/16/70 - 7
The Isaac Hayes Movement...
Isaac Hayes

6/20/70 - 12
ABC...*Jackson 5*

9/26/70 - 2
Diana Ross...*Diana Ross*

10/10/70 - 10
Third Album...*Jackson 5*

12/19/70 - 1
Greatest Hits...
Sly & The Family Stone

12/26/70 - 11
To Be Continued...*Isaac Hayes*

2/6/71 - 5
Curtis...*Curtis Mayfield*

4/10/71 - 3
Live In Cook County Jail...
B.B. King

5/8/71 - 6
Maybe Tomorrow...*Jackson 5*

6/19/71 - 5
Aretha Live At Fillmore West...
Aretha Franklin

7/24/71 - 9
What's Going On...*Marvin Gaye*

9/25/71 - 14
Shaft...
Isaac Hayes/Soundtrack

1/1/72 - 2
There's A Riot Goin' On...
Sly & The Family Stone

1/15/72 - 7
Black Moses...*Isaac Hayes*

3/4/72 - 2
Solid Rock...*The Temptations*

3/18/72 - 10
Let's Stay Together...*Al Green*

5/27/72 - 2
First Take...*Roberta Flack*

6/10/72 - 5
A Lonely Man...*The Chi-Lites*

7/15/72 - 6
Still Bill...*Bill Withers*

10/14/72 - 6
Superfly...
Curtis Mayfield/Soundtrack

11/25/72 - 1
All Directions...
The Temptations

12/2/72 - 5
I'm Still In Love With You...
Al Green

1973

1/6/73 - 2
360 Degrees Of Billy Paul...
Billy Paul

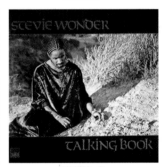

1/20/73 - 3
Talking Book...*Stevie Wonder*

2/10/73 - 7
The World Is A Ghetto...*War*

3/31/73 - 2
Wattstax: The Living Word...
Soundtrack

4/14/73 - 2
Neither One Of Us...
Gladys Knight & The Pips

4/28/73 - 2
Masterpiece...*The Temptations*

5/12/73 - 3
Spinners...*Spinners*

6/2/73 - 1
Birth Day...*The New Birth*

6/9/73 - 2
Call Me...*Al Green*

6/23/73 - 2
Live At The Sahara Tahoe...
Isaac Hayes

7/7/73 - 2
I've Got So Much To Give...
Barry White

7/21/73 - 2
Back To The World...
Curtis Mayfield

8/4/73 - 3
Fresh...*Sly & The Family Stone*

8/25/73 - 2
Touch Me In The Morning...
Diana Ross

9/8/73 - 2
Innervisions...*Stevie Wonder*

9/22/73 - 1
Deliver The Word...*War*

9/29/73 - 11
Let's Get It On...*Marvin Gaye*

1973 / 1974

1974

12/15/73 - 7
Imagination...
Gladys Knight & The Pips

2/2/74 - 2
Stone Gon'...*Barry White*

2/16/74 - 5
Ship Ahoy...*The O'Jays*

2/23/74 - 1
Livin' For You...*Al Green*

3/16/74 - 6
Love Is The Message...*MFSB*

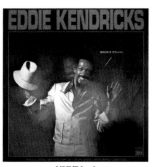

4/27/74 - 1
Boogie Down!...*Eddie Kendricks*

5/4/74 - 2
The Payback...*James Brown*

5/18/74 - 1
Let Me In Your Life...
Aretha Franklin

5/25/74 - 1
Open Our Eyes...
Earth, Wind & Fire

6/1/74 - 1
Mighty Love...*Spinners*

6/22/74 - 2
War Live!...*War*

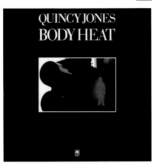

7/6/74 - 1
Body Heat...*Quincy Jones*

7/13/74 - 1
Claudine...
Gladys Knight & The Pips

7/20/74 - 6
Skin Tight...*Ohio Players*

8/31/74 - 2
Marvin Gaye Live!...
Marvin Gaye

9/7/74 - 4
That Nigger's Crazy...
Richard Pryor

10/5/74 - 8
Fulfillingness' First Finale...
Stevie Wonder

11/16/74 - 1
Live It Up...
The Isley Brothers

11/23/74 - 2
Can't Get Enough...*Barry White*

12/28/74 - 1
I Feel A Song...
Gladys Knight & The Pips

1975

1/4/75 - 5
Fire...*Ohio Players*

2/8/75 - 1
**Kung Fu Fighting And Other Great
Love Songs**...*Carl Douglas*

2/15/75 - 1
New And Improved...*Spinners*

2/22/75 - 1
Do It ('Til You're Satisfied)...
B.T. Express

3/1/75 - 3
AWB...*Average White Band*

3/22/75 - 1
Al Green Explores Your Mind...
Al Green

3/29/75 - 3
Perfect Angel...
Minnie Riperton

4/19/75 - 5
That's The Way Of The World...
Earth, Wind & Fire

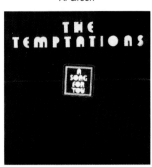

5/3/75 - 1
A Song For You...
The Temptations

5/10/75 - 1
To Be True...
Harold Melvin & The Blue Notes

5/17/75 - 1
Mister Magic...
Grover Washington, Jr.

5/24/75 - 1
Sun Goddess...*Ramsey Lewis*

5/31/75 - 1
**Just Another Way To Say I Love
You**...*Barry White*

6/7/75 - 2
Survival...*The O'Jays*

7/12/75 - 1
Disco Baby...*Van McCoy*

7/19/75 - 4
The Heat Is On...
The Isley Brothers

8/9/75 - 2
Chocolate Chip...*Isaac Hayes*

8/23/75 - 1
Cut The Cake...
Average White Band

8/30/75 - 1
Why Can't We Be Friends?...*War*

9/6/75 - 2
Non-Stop...*B.T. Express*

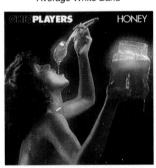

9/27/75 - 3
Honey...*Ohio Players*

10/11/75 - 2
Is It Something I Said?...
Richard Pryor

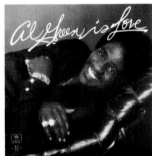

11/1/75 - 2
Al Green Is Love...*Al Green*

11/15/75 - 1
KC And The Sunshine Band...
KC And The Sunshine Band

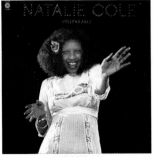

11/22/75 - 1
Inseparable...*Natalie Cole*

11/29/75 - 1
Save Me...*Silver Convention*

12/6/75 - 2
Let's Do It Again...
The Staple Singers

12/20/75 - 1
Feels So Good...
Grover Washington, Jr.

12/27/75 - 1
Family Reunion...*The O'Jays*

1976

1/3/76 - 6
Gratitude...*Earth, Wind & Fire*

1/24/76 - 2
Wake Up Everybody...
Harold Melvin & The Blue Notes

2/28/76 - 6
Rufus Featuring Chaka Khan...
Rufus featuring Chaka Khan

4/10/76 - 2
Eargasm...*Johnnie Taylor*

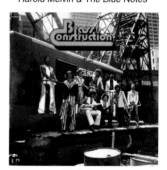

4/24/76 - 3
Brass Construction...
Brass Construction

5/15/76 - 1
I Want You...*Marvin Gaye*

5/22/76 - 6
Breezin'...*George Benson*

5/29/76 - 4
Look Out For #1...
The Brothers Johnson

6/26/76 - 1
Harvest For The World...
The Isley Brothers

7/24/76 - 1
Contradiction...*Ohio Players*

7/31/76 - 1
Sparkle...*Aretha Franklin*

8/21/76 - 1
All Things In Time...*Lou Rawls*

8/28/76 - 6
Hot On The Tracks...*Commodores*

9/11/76 - 1
Wild Cherry...*Wild Cherry*

10/16/76 - 20
Songs In The Key Of Life...
Stevie Wonder

1977

1/8/77 - 1
Good High...*Brick*

3/12/77 - 3
Ask Rufus...
Rufus Featuring Chaka Khan

4/2/77 - 3
Unpredictable...*Natalie Cole*

4/23/77 - 1
Ahh...The Name Is Bootsy, Baby!...
Bootsy's Rubber Band

4/30/77 - 2
Marvin Gaye Live At The London Palladium...*Marvin Gaye*

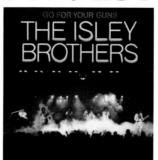

5/14/77 - 2
Go For Your Guns...
The Isley Brothers

5/21/77 - 8
Commodores...*Commodores*

7/23/77 - 7
Rejoice...*Emotions*

8/6/77 - 3
The Floaters...*Floaters*

10/1/77 - 3
Rose Royce II/In Full Bloom...
Rose Royce

10/8/77 - 1
Something To Love...*L.T.D.*

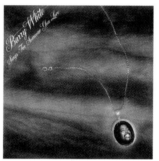

10/15/77 - 5
Barry White Sings For Someone You Love...*Barry White*

11/12/77 - 2
Brick...*Brick*

12/17/77 - 9
All 'N All...
Earth, Wind & Fire

2/18/78 - 6
Saturday Night Fever...
Bee Gees/Soundtrack

3/25/78 - 3
Bootsy? Player Of The Year...
Bootsy's Rubber Band

4/15/78 - 1
Street Player...
Rufus/Chaka Khan

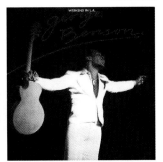

4/29/78 - 2
Weekend In L.A....
George Benson

5/13/78 - 3
Showdown...*The Isley Brothers*

6/3/78 - 3
So Full Of Love...*The O'Jays*

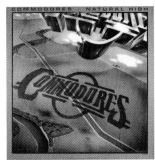

6/24/78 - 8
Natural High...*Commodores*

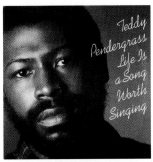

8/12/78 - 2
Life Is A Song Worth Singing...
Teddy Pendergrass

9/2/78 - 7
Blam!!...*The Brothers Johnson*

10/21/78 - 1
Is It Still Good To Ya...
Ashford & Simpson

10/28/78 - 4
One Nation Under A Groove...
Funkadelic

11/25/78 - 3
Barry White The Man...
Barry White

12/16/78 - 11
C'est Chic...*Chic*

1979

3/3/79 - 8
2 Hot!...*Peaches & Herb*

3/31/79 - 1
Instant Funk...*Instant Funk*

4/7/79 - 7
We Are Family...*Sister Sledge*

6/23/79 - 3
Bad Girls...*Donna Summer*

7/14/79 - 1
I Am...*Earth, Wind & Fire*

7/21/79 - 8
Teddy...*Teddy Pendergrass*

9/15/79 - 3
Midnight Magic...*Commodores*

10/6/79 - 16
Off The Wall...*Michael Jackson*

10/27/79 - 2
Ladies' Night...
Kool & The Gang

12/22/79 - 2
Masterjam...
Rufus & Chaka Khan

2/23/80 - 8
The Whispers...*The Whispers*

4/19/80 - 2
Light Up The Night...
The Brothers Johnson

5/3/80 - 5
Go All The Way...
The Isley Brothers

6/7/80 - 5
Let's Get Serious...
Jermaine Jackson

7/12/80 - 2
Cameosis...*Cameo*

7/26/80 - 8
Diana...*Diana Ross*

9/20/80 - 4
Give Me The Night...
George Benson

10/18/80 - 1
Love Approach...*Tom Browne*

10/25/80 - 2
Zapp...*Zapp*

11/8/80 - 2
Triumph...*The Jacksons*

11/22/80 - 13
Hotter Than July...
Stevie Wonder

1981

1981 / 1982

2/21/81 - 6
The Gap Band III...
The Gap Band

3/7/81 - 2
The Two Of Us...
Yarbrough & Peoples

4/18/81 - 5
Being With You...
Smokey Robinson

5/23/81 - 2
A Woman Needs Love...
Ray Parker Jr.

6/6/81 - 20
Street Songs...*Rick James*

10/24/81 - 2
Breakin' Away...*Al Jarreau*

11/7/81 - 1
The Many Facets Of Roger...
Roger

11/14/81 - 1
Never Too Much...
Luther Vandross

11/21/81 - 1
Something Special...
Kool & The Gang

11/28/81 - 11
Raise!...*Earth, Wind & Fire*

2/13/82 - 4
Skyy Line...*Skyy*

2/20/82 - 5
The Poet...*Bobby Womack*

4/17/82 - 1
Love Is Where You Find It...
The Whispers

4/24/82 - 2
Friends...*Shalamar*

5/8/82 - 3
Brilliance...*Atlantic Starr*

5/29/82 - 1
The Other Woman...
Ray Parker Jr.

6/5/82 - 3
Stevie Wonder's Original
Musiquarium I...*Stevie Wonder*

6/19/82 - 1
Keep It Live...*Dazz Band*

7/3/82 - 9
Gap Band IV...*The Gap Band*

9/4/82 - 7
Jump To It...*Aretha Franklin*

10/23/82 - 2
Get Loose...
Evelyn King

11/6/82 - 3
Forever, For Always, For Love...
Luther Vandross

11/27/82 - 1
Lionel Richie...*Lionel Richie*

12/4/82 - 8
Midnight Love...*Marvin Gaye*

1/29/83 - 37
Thriller...*Michael Jackson*

7/23/83 - 1
Between The Sheets...
The Isley Brothers

9/17/83 - 10
Cold Blooded...*Rick James*

11/26/83 - 23
Can't Slow Down...
Lionel Richie

4/14/84 - 2
Busy Body...*Luther Vandross*

4/28/84 - 2
She's Strange...*Cameo*

7/7/84 - 1
Jermaine Jackson...
Jermaine Jackson

7/14/84 - 1
Lady...*One Way*

7/21/84 - 3
Private Dancer...*Tina Turner*

7/28/84 - 19
Purple Rain...*Prince and the Revolution/Soundtrack*

12/8/84 - 4
The Woman In Red...
Stevie Wonder/Soundtrack

1/5/85 - 5
New Edition...*New Edition*

2/9/85 - 4
Solid...*Ashford & Simpson*

3/9/85 - 2
Gap Band VI...*The Gap Band*

4/6/85 - 3
Nightshift...*Commodores*

4/27/85 - 1
Can't Stop The Love...
Maze Featuring Frankie Beverly

5/4/85 - 7
The Night I Fell In Love...
Luther Vandross

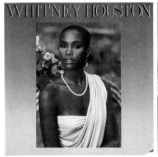

6/22/85 - 6
Whitney Houston...
Whitney Houston

6/29/85 - 14
Rock Me Tonight...
Freddie Jackson

11/9/85 - 12
In Square Circle...
Stevie Wonder

1986 / 1987

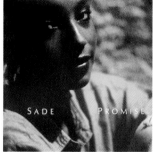

2/1/86 - 11
Promise...*Sade*

4/19/86 - 8
Control...*Janet Jackson*

6/14/86 - 8
Winner In You...*Patti LaBelle*

8/9/86 - 1
Love Zone...*Billy Ocean*

8/16/86 - 7
Raising Hell...*Run DMC*

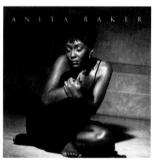

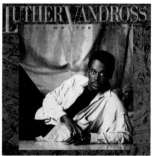

9/20/86 - 3
Rapture...*Anita Baker*

10/25/86 - 5
Word Up!...*Cameo*

11/29/86 - 2
Give Me The Reason...
Luther Vandross

12/6/86 - 26
Just Like The First Time...
Freddie Jackson

6/6/87 - 3
Jody Watley...*Jody Watley*

7/4/87 - 1
One Heartbeat...
Smokey Robinson

7/11/87 - 11
Bigger And Deffer...*L.L. Cool J*

9/5/87 - 1
If I Were Your Woman...
Stephanie Mills

10/3/87 - 18
Bad...*Michael Jackson*

12/19/87 - 7
Characters...*Stevie Wonder*

1988

2/27/88 - 2
All Our Love...
Gladys Knight & The Pips

3/19/88 - 3
Make It Last Forever...
Keith Sweat

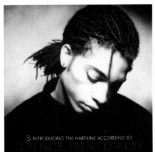

4/30/88 - 3 — Introducing The
Hardline According To Terence
Trent D'Arby...*Terence Trent D'Arby*

5/21/88 - 6
Faith...*George Michael*

7/2/88 - 7
In Effect Mode...*Al B. Sure!*

8/20/88 - 3
Strictly Business...*EPMD*

93

9/10/88 - 11
Don't Be Cruel...*Bobby Brown*

9/24/88 - 1
It Takes A Nation Of Millions To
Hold Us Back...*Public Enemy*

10/15/88 - 1
Don't Let Love Slip Away...
Freddie Jackson

11/19/88 - 8
Giving You The Best That I Got...
Anita Baker

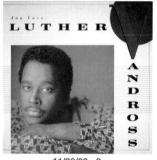

11/26/88 - 2
Any Love...*Luther Vandross*

1989

1/28/89 - 7
Karyn White...*Karyn White*

4/8/89 - 1
Let's Get It Started...
M.C. Hammer

4/15/89 - 5
Guy...*Guy*

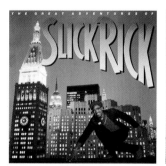

5/13/89 - 4
The Great Adventures Of Slick
Rick...*Slick Rick*

5/27/89 - 5
3 Feet High And Rising...
De La Soul

7/22/89 - 5
Walking With A Panther...
L.L. Cool J

8/26/89 - 2
Big Tyme...*Heavy D. & The Boyz*

9/2/89 - 1
Keep On Movin'...*Soul II Soul*

9/16/89 - 2
Unfinished Business...*EPMD*

9/30/89 - 2
No One Can Do It Better...
The D.O.C.

10/14/89 - 11
Tender Lover...*Babyface*

11/11/89 - 1
Silky Soul...
Maze Featuring Frankie Beverly

11/18/89 - 3
**Janet Jackson's Rhythm Nation
1814**...*Janet Jackson*

12/2/89 - 1
Stay With Me...*Regina Belle*

1990

1/27/90 - 12
Back On The Block...
Quincy Jones

4/28/90 - 29
Please Hammer Don't Hurt 'Em...
M.C. Hammer

6/2/90 - 1
Poison...*Bell Biv DeVoe*

6/30/90 - 3
Johnny Gill...*Johnny Gill*

8/25/90 - 1
I'll Give All My Love To You...
Keith Sweat

12/22/90 - 8
I'm Your Baby Tonight...
Whitney Houston

1991

2/2/91 - 3
The Future...*Guy*

2/23/91 - 2
Do Me Again...*Freddie Jackson*

3/23/91 - 2
Business As Usual...*EPMD*

4/6/91 - 2
Ralph Tresvant...
Ralph Tresvant

4/20/91 - 1
Hi-Five...*Hi-Five*

4/27/91 - 8
New Jack City...
Soundtrack

6/22/91 - 5
Power Of Love...
Luther Vandross

7/6/91 - 2
Make Time For Love...
Keith Washington

8/3/91 - 2
Music From The Movie Jungle
Fever...*Stevie Wonder*

8/24/91 - 2
Cooleyhighharmony...
Boyz II Men

9/7/91 - 4
Boyz N The Hood...
Soundtrack

10/5/91 - 2
Can You Stop The Rain...
Peabo Bryson

10/19/91 - 1
Good Woman...*Gladys Knight*

10/26/91 - 2
Different Lifestyles...
BeBe & CeCe Winans

11/9/91 - 1
As Raw As Ever...*Shabba Ranks*

11/16/91 - 2
Forever My Lady...*Jodeci*

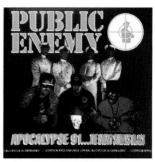

11/23/91 - 1
Apocalypse 91...The Enemy Strikes
Black...*Public Enemy*

12/7/91 - 1
Diamonds And Pearls...
Prince & The New Power Generation

12/14/91 - 3
Death Certificate...*Ice Cube*

1992

1/4/92 - 12
Dangerous...*Michael Jackson*

2/1/92 - 3
Keep It Comin'...*Keith Sweat*

4/18/92 - 2
Private Line...*Gerald Levert*

5/2/92 - 1
The Comfort Zone...
Vanessa Williams

5/9/92 - 2
Funky Divas...*En Vogue*

5/23/92 - 6
Totally Krossed Out...
Kris Kross

6/20/92 - 5
Dead Serious...*DAS EFX*

8/8/92 - 8
Boomerang...*Soundtrack*

10/3/92 - 7
What's The 411?...
Mary J. Blige

11/7/92 - 2
Bobby...*Bobby Brown*

12/5/92 - 1
The Predator...*Ice Cube*

12/12/92 - 8
The Bodyguard...
Whitney Houston/Soundtrack

2/6/93 - 8
The Chronic...*Dr. Dre*

3/13/93 - 2
19 Naughty III...
Naughty By Nature

3/27/93 - 2
Till Death Do Us Part...
Geto Boys

4/10/93 - 1
Lose Control...*Silk*

4/17/93 - 2
14 Shots To The Dome...
LL Cool J

5/22/93 - 1
Down With The King...
Run-DMC

5/29/93 - 1
Fever For Da Flavor...*H-Town*

6/5/93 - 3
janet....*Janet Jackson*

6/26/93 - 6
Menace II Society...
Soundtrack

8/7/93 - 4
Black Sunday...*Cypress Hill*

9/4/93 - 2
The World Is Yours...*Scarface*

9/18/93 - 2
Music Box...*Mariah Carey*

10/2/93 - 3
Toni Braxton...*Toni Braxton*

10/16/93 - 2
187 He Wrote...*Spice 1*

11/6/93 - 1
It's On (Dr. Dre) 187um Killa...
Eazy-E

11/13/93 - 2
Get In Where You Fit In...
Too $hort

11/27/93 - 1
Midnight Marauders...
A Tribe Called Quest

12/4/93 - 1
Shock Of The Hour...*MC Ren*

12/11/93 - 5
Doggy Style...*Snoop Doggy Dogg*

12/25/93 - 1
Lethal Injection...*Ice Cube*

1/22/94 - 2
Diary Of A Mad Band...*Jodeci*

2/5/94 - 9
12 Play...*R. Kelly*

4/9/94 - 10
Above The Rim...
Soundtrack

6/11/94 - 1
Nuttin' But Love...
Heavy D & The Boyz

6/25/94 - 3
Regulate...G Funk Era...
Warren G

7/16/94 - 2
Get Up On It...*Keith Sweat*

7/30/94 - 1
Funkdafied...*Da Brat*

8/6/94 - 5
We Come Strapped...
MC Eiht Featuring CMW

9/10/94 - 1
Changing Faces...
Changing Faces

9/17/94 - 2
II...*Boyz II Men*

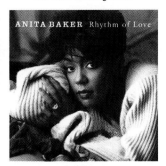

10/1/94 - 4
Rhythm Of Love...*Anita Baker*

10/29/94 - 1
Jason's Lyric...
Soundtrack

11/5/94 - 1
Murder Was The Case...
Soundtrack

11/26/94 - 1
The Icon Is Love...*Barry White*

12/3/94 - 1
Tical...*Method Man*

12/10/94 - 1
Dare Iz A Darkside...*Redman*

12/17/94 - 8
My Life...*Mary J. Blige*

12/24/94 - 3
Miracles - The Holiday Album...
Kenny G

1995

2/11/95 - 2
Cocktails...*Too Short*

3/11/95 - 2
Safe + Sound...*DJ Quik*

4/1/95 - 4
Me Against The World...*2 Pac*

4/29/95 - 6
Friday...*Soundtrack*

6/10/95 - 1
Tales From The Hood...
Soundtrack

6/17/95 - 3
Poverty's Paradise...
Naughty By Nature

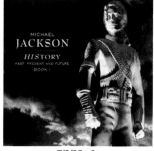

7/8/95 - 2
HIStory: Past, Present And Future -
Book I...*Michael Jackson*

7/22/95 - 2
Operation Stackola...*Luniz*

8/5/95 - 1
The Show - The After-Party - The Hotel...*Jodeci*

8/12/95 - 3
E. 1999 Eternal...
Bone thugs-n-harmony

9/2/95 - 6
The Show...*Soundtrack*

10/14/95 - 1
4,5,6...*Kool G Rap*

10/21/95 - 1
Daydream...*Mariah Carey*

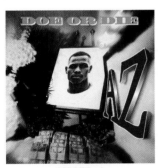

10/28/95 - 1
Doe Or Die...*AZ*

11/4/95 - 2
Dead Presidents...
Soundtrack

11/18/95 - 2
Dogg Food...*Tha Dogg Pound*

12/2/95 - 2
R. Kelly...*R. Kelly*

12/16/95 - 10
Waiting To Exhale...
Soundtrack

1996

1996

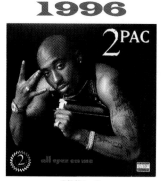

2/17/96 - 1
Str8 Off Tha Streetz Of
Muthaphukkin Compton...*Eazy-E*

3/2/96 - 3
All Eyez On Me...*2Pac*

3/23/96 - 8
The Score...*Fugees*

4/13/96 - 1
The Coming...*Busta Rhymes*

4/20/96 - 1
The Resurrection...
The Geto Boys

5/11/96 - 1
Sunset Park...*Soundtrack*

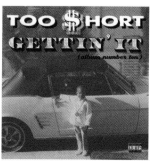

6/8/96 - 2
Gettin' It (Album Number Ten)...
Too $hort

6/22/96 - 1
Legal Drug Money...*Lost Boyz*

6/29/96 - 1
The Nutty Professor...
Soundtrack

7/6/96 - 1
Secrets...*Toni Braxton*

7/13/96 - 1
Keith Sweat...*Keith Sweat*

7/20/96 - 7
It Was Written...*Nas*

8/17/96 - 1
Beats, Rhymes And Life...
A Tribe Called Quest

9/14/96 - 2
ATLiens...*OutKast*

9/28/96 - 1
Home Again...*New Edition*

10/5/96 - 5
Another Level...*BLACKstreet*

11/9/96 - 1
Bow Down...*Westside Connection*

11/16/96 - 1
Ironman...*Ghostface Killah*

11/23/96 - 6
**The Don Killuminati - The 7 Day
Theory...***Makaveli*

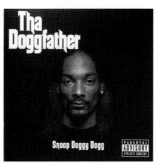

11/30/96 - 1
Tha Doggfather...
Snoop Doggy Dogg

12/7/96 - 1
Hell On Earth...*Mobb Deep*

12/28/96 - 1
Muddy Waters...*Redman*

1997

1/4/97 - 2
The Preacher's Wife...
Whitney Houston/Soundtrack

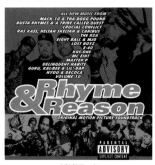

2/1/97 - 1
Rhyme & Reason...
Soundtrack

2/15/97 - 2
Gridlock'd...*Soundtrack*

3/1/97 - 4
Baduizm...*Erykah Badu*

3/29/97 - 2
The Untouchable...*Scarface*

4/12/97 - 4
Life After Death...
The Notorious B.I.G.

5/10/97 - 4
Share My World...*Mary J. Blige*

6/7/97 - 1
I'm Bout It...*Soundtrack*

6/14/97 - 5 — God's Property...
*God's Property From Kirk Franklin's
Nu Nation*

6/21/97 - 2
Wu-Tang Forever...*Wu-Tang Clan*

8/2/97 - 1
Supa Dupa Fly...
Missy "Misdemeanor" Elliott

8/9/97 - 5
No Way Out...
Puff Daddy & The Family

8/16/97 - 1
The Art Of War...
Bone thugs-n-harmony

9/20/97 - 2
Ghetto D...*Master P*

10/4/97 - 1
When Disaster Strikes......
Busta Rhymes

10/11/97 - 1
Evolution...*Boyz II Men*

10/18/97 - 1
Soul Food...*Soundtrack*

10/25/97 - 2
Gang Related...
Soundtrack

11/8/97 - 1
The Firm - The Album...
The Firm

11/15/97 - 1
Harlem World...*Mase*

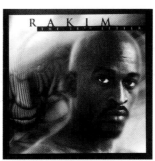

11/22/97 - 1
The 18th Letter...*Rakim*

11/29/97 - 1
Unpredictable...*Mystikal*

12/6/97 - 3
Live...*Erykah Badu*

12/13/97 - 2
R U Still Down? [Remember Me]...
2Pac

107

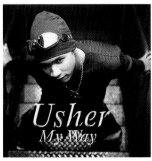

1/10/98 - 3
My Way...*Usher*

1/31/98 - 1
Money, Power & Respect...
The Lox

2/7/98 - 1 — **All I Have In This World,
Are...My Balls And My Word**...
Young Bleed

2/14/98 - 3
Anytime...*Brian McKnight*

3/7/98 - 2
Charge It 2 Da Game...
Silkk The Shocker

3/21/98 - 2
My Homies...*Scarface*

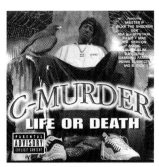

4/4/98 - 1
Life Or Death...*C-Murder*

4/11/98 - 1
The Pillage...*Cappadonna*

4/18/98 - 1
Moment Of Truth...*Gang Starr*

4/25/98 - 3
I Got The Hook-Up!...
Soundtrack

5/16/98 - 2
Capital Punishment...
Big Punisher

5/23/98 - 1
There's One In Every Family...
Fiend

6/6/98 - 2
It's Dark And Hell Is Hot...
DMX

6/20/98 - 4
MP Da Last Don...*Master P*

7/18/98 - 1
El Niño...*Def Squad*

7/25/98 - 1
Am I My Brothers Keeper...
Kane & Abel

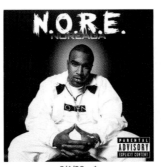

8/1/98 - 1
N.O.R.E.....*Noreaga*

8/8/98 - 2 — Jermaine Dupri
**Presents Life In 1472 - The Original
Soundtrack**...*Jermaine Dupri*

8/22/98 - 3
**Da Game Is To Be Sold, Not To Be
Told**...*Snoop Dogg*

9/12/98 - 6
The Miseducation Of Lauryn Hill...
Lauryn Hill

10/17/98 - 6
Vol. 2...Hard Knock Life...
Jay-Z

11/28/98 - 1
R....*R. Kelly*

12/5/98 - 1
Tical 2000: Judgement Day...
Method Man

12/12/98 - 2
Greatest Hits...*2Pac*

12/26/98 - 1
Doc's Da Name 2000...*Redman*

1999

1/2/99 - 1
Ghetto Fabulous...*Mystikal*

1/9/99 - 4
Flesh Of My Flesh Blood Of My Blood...*DMX*

2/6/99 - 1
Made Man...*Silkk The Shocker*

2/13/99 - 2
Chyna Doll...*Foxy Brown*

3/6/99 - 1
Da Next Level...*Mr. Servon*

3/13/99 - 4
Fanmail...*TLC*

3/27/99 - 1
Bossalinie...*C-Murder*

4/10/99 - 1
The Slim Shady LP...*Eminem*

4/24/99 - 3
I Am......*Nas*

5/15/99 - 2
Ruff Ryders - Ryde Or Die Vol. I...
Ruff Ryders

5/29/99 - 1
No Limit Top Dogg...*Snoop Dogg*

6/5/99 - 1
In Our Lifetime...
Eightball & MJG

6/12/99 - 1
The Art Of Storytelling...
Slick Rick

6/19/99 - 3
Venni Vetti Vecci...*Ja Rule*

7/10/99 - 1
Da Real World...
Missy "Misdemeanor" Elliott

7/17/99 - 1
Beneath The Surface...
GZA/Genius

7/24/99 - 1
Street Life...*Fiend*

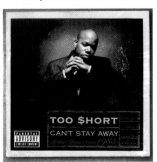

7/31/99 - 2
Can't Stay Away...*Too $hort*

8/14/99 - 1
Guerilla Warfare...*Hot Boy$*

8/21/99 - 1
Coming Of Age...*Memphis Bleek*

8/28/99 - 1
Violator - The Album...
Various Artists

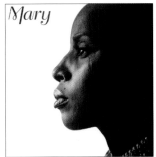

9/4/99 - 3
Mary...*Mary J. Blige*

9/11/99 - 1
Forever...*Puff Daddy*

10/2/99 - 4
Ruff Ryders' First Lady...*Eve*

10/16/99 - 2
Blackout!...*Method Man Redman*

11/13/99 - 1
Only God Can Judge Me...
Master P

11/20/99 - 2
Tha Block Is Hot...*Lil Wayne*

12/4/99 - 4
2001...*Dr. Dre*

12/25/99 - 1
Born Again...
The Notorious B.I.G.

2000

1/1/00 - 1
Tha G-Code...*Juvenile*

1/8/00 - 2
...And Then There Was X...*DMX*

1/15/00 - 2
**Vol. 3...Life And Times Of
S. Carter**...*Jay-Z*

2/5/00 - 1
J.E. Heartbreak...*Jagged Edge*

2/12/00 - 4
Voodoo...*D'Angelo*

3/18/00 - 1
BTNHRESURRECTION...
Bone thugs-n-harmony

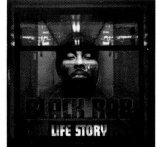

3/25/00 - 2
Life Story...*Black Rob*

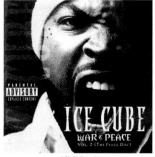

4/8/00 - 1
War & Peace Vol. 2 (The Peace Disc)...*Ice Cube*

4/15/00 - 1
Romeo Must Die...
Soundtrack

4/22/00 - 1
Yeeeah Baby...*Big Pun*

4/29/00 - 1
Unrestricted...*Da Brat*

5/6/00 - 1
My Name Is Joe...*Joe*

5/13/00 - 1
The Heat...*Toni Braxton*

5/20/00 - 2
Goodfellas...*504 Boyz*

6/3/00 - 1
I Got That Work...*Big Tymers*

6/10/00 - 4
The Marshall Mathers LP...
Eminem

7/8/00 - 1
Anarchy...*Busta Rhymes*

7/15/00 - 1
The Notorious KIM...*Lil' Kim*

7/22/00 - 1
Ruff Ryders - Ryde Or Die Vol. II...
Ruff Ryders

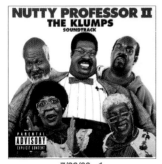

7/29/00 - 1
Nutty Professor II: The Klumps...
Soundtrack

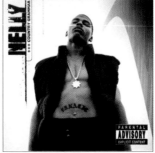

8/5/00 - 6
Country Grammar...*Nelly*

9/16/00 - 1
Backstage Mixtape...*DJ Clue*

9/23/00 - 1
Trapped In Crime...*C-Murder*

9/30/00 - 2 — G.O.A.T. Featuring
James T. Smith The Greatest Of All
Time...*LL Cool J*

10/14/00 - 2
Let's Get Ready...*Mystikal*

10/28/00 - 3
Rule 3:36...*Ja Rule*

11/18/00 - 1
The Dynasty Roc La Familia
(2000 -)...*Jay-Z*

11/25/00 - 3
TP-2.com...*R. Kelly*

12/9/00 - 1
The W...*Wu-Tang Clan*

12/23/00 - 1
The Understanding...
Memphis Bleek

12/30/00 - 1
Restless...*Xzibit*

2001

1/6/01 - 4
Tha Last Meal...*Snoop Dogg*

2/3/01 - 5
Hotshot...*Shaggy*

2/10/01 - 1
J.Lo...*Jennifer Lopez*

3/17/01 - 1
The Professional 2...*DJ Clue?*

3/24/01 - 1
Scorpion...*Eve*

3/31/01 - 1
Force Of Nature...*Tank*

4/7/01 - 1
Part III...*One Twelve*

4/14/01 - 4
Until The End Of Time...*2Pac*

5/12/01 - 1
All For You...*Janet Jackson*

5/19/01 - 2
Survivor...*Destiny's Child*

6/2/01 - 2
Miss E... So Addictive...
Missy "Misdemeanor" Elliott

6/9/01 - 1
Malpractice...*Redman*

6/23/01 - 2
Free City...*St. Lunatics*

7/7/01 - 1
Devil's Night...*D12*

7/14/01 - 6
Songs In A Minor...*Alicia Keys*

8/25/01 - 2
Eternal...*The Isley Brothers*

9/8/01 - 1
Now...*Maxwell*

9/15/01 - 2
No More Drama...*Mary J. Blige*

9/29/01 - 3
The Blueprint...*Jay-Z*

10/20/01 - 3
Pain Is Love...*Ja Rule*

11/10/01 - 1
The Great Depression...*DMX*

11/17/01 - 4
Invincible...*Michael Jackson*

12/15/01 - 3
Word Of Mouf...*Ludacris*

12/29/01 - 1
Infamy...*Mobb Deep*

2002

1/5/02 - 6
Stillmatic...*Nas*

2/16/02 - 1
State Property...
Soundtrack

2/23/02 - 1
J To Tha L-O! The Remixes...
Jennifer Lopez

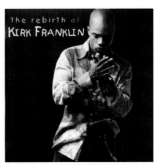

3/9/02 - 2
The Rebirth Of Kirk Franklin...
Kirk Franklin

3/23/02 - 1
Full Moon...*Brandy*

3/30/02 - 1
B2K...*B2K*

4/6/02 - 2
The Best Of Both Worlds...
R. Kelly & Jay-Z

4/20/02 - 4
Ashanti...*Ashanti*

5/18/02 - 1
Hood Rich...*Big Tymers*

5/25/02 - 1
JUSLISEN (Just Listen)...*Musiq*

6/1/02 - 1
Come Home With Me...*Cam'ron*

6/8/02 - 6
The Eminem Show...*Eminem*

7/13/02 - 5
Nellyville...*Nelly*

8/10/02 - 1
500 Degreez...*Lil Wayne*

8/24/02 - 2
The Fix...*Scarface*

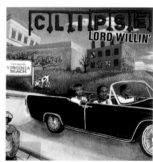

9/7/02 - 2
Lord Willin'...*Clipse*

9/14/02 - 1
Eve-olution...*Eve*

10/5/02 - 1
Golden Grain...
Disturbing Tha Peace

10/12/02 - 1
Voyage To India...*India.Arie*

10/19/02 - 2
Man vs Machine...*Xzibit*

11/2/02 - 2
10...*LL Cool J*

11/16/02 - 2
8 Mile...*Soundtrack*

11/30/02 - 2
The Blueprint 2: The Gift And The Curse...*Jay-Z*

12/14/02 - 2
Better Dayz...*2Pac*

12/28/02 - 7
I Care 4 U...*Aaliyah*

1/4/03 - 1
God's Son...*Nas*

2/22/03 - 8
Get Rich Or Die Tryin'...
50 Cent

3/8/03 - 1
Chocolate Factory...*R. Kelly*

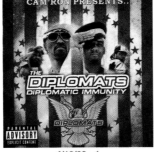

4/12/03 - 1
Diplomatic Immunity...
Cam'ron Presents The Diplomats

4/26/03 - 1
The Senior...*Ginuwine*

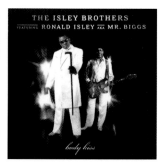

5/3/03 - 1
The New Breed...*50 Cent*

5/17/03 - 1
AttenCHUN!...*Bone Crusher*

5/24/03 - 3 — Body Kiss...
The Isley Brothers Featuring Ronald Isley AKA Mr. Biggs

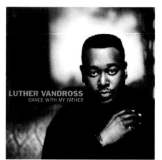

6/7/03 - 1
Mississippi: The Album...
David Banner

6/21/03 - 1
2 Fast 2 Furious...
Soundtrack

6/28/03 - 2
Dance With My Father...
Luther Vandross

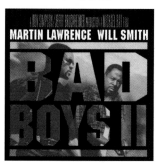

7/12/03 - 1
Dangerously In Love...*Beyoncé*

7/19/03 - 2
Chapter II...*Ashanti*

8/2/03 - 4
Bad Boys II...*Soundtrack*

8/30/03 - 1
State Property Presents: The Chain Gang Vol. II...*Various Artists*

9/6/03 - 1
The Neptunes Present...Clones...
Various Artists

9/13/03 - 2
Love & Life...*Mary J. Blige*

2003 / 2004 R&B

9/27/03 - 1
Drankin' Patnaz...*Youngbloodz*

10/4/03 - 1
Grand Champ...*DMX*

10/11/03 - 1
Speakerboxxx/The Love Below...
OutKast

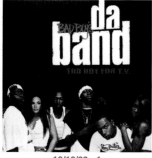

10/18/03 - 1
Too Hot For T.V....
Bad Boy's Da Band

10/25/03 - 2
Chicken*N*Beer...*Ludacris*

11/1/03 - 1
Hard...*Jagged Edge*

11/15/03 - 1
Stroke Of Genius...
Gerald Levert

11/22/03 - 1
Blood In My Eye...*Ja Rule*

11/29/03 - 3
The Black Album...*Jay-Z*

12/20/03 - 6
The Diary Of Alicia Keys...
Alicia Keys

2004

1/31/04 - 2
Soulful...*Ruben Studdard*

2004

2/14/04 - 2
Kamikaze...*Twista*

2/28/04 - 2
The College Dropout...
Kanye West

3/13/04 - 1+
Tough Luv...*Young Gunz*

The All-Time #1 R&B Albums

❶ **Thriller**...*Michael Jackson*
37 weeks at #1 — Year: 1983

❷ **Please Hammer Don't Hurt
'Em**...*M.C. Hammer*
29 weeks at #1 — Year: 1990

❸ **Just Like The First Time**...
Freddie Jackson
26 weeks at #1 — Year: 1986

❹ **Can't Slow Down**...*Lionel Richie*
23 weeks at #1 — Year: 1983

❺ **Songs In The Key Of Life**...
Stevie Wonder
20 weeks at #1 — Year: 1976

❻ **Street Songs**...*Rick James*
20 weeks at #1 — Year: 1981

The #1 Country Albums

1964-2004

This section displays, in chronological order, full-color representations of the 373 albums that hit #1 on *Billboard's* Country Albums chart from January 11, 1964 through March 13, 2004. The chart is currently named Top Country Albums.

The date an album first hit #1 is listed below each album's picture. The total weeks the album held the #1 position is listed to the right of the date.

Billboard has not published an issue for the last week of the year since 1976. For the years 1976 through 1991, *Billboard* considered the charts listed in the last published issue of the year to be "frozen" and all chart positions remained the same for the unpublished week. This frozen chart data is included in our tabulations. Since 1992, *Billboard* has compiled the Top Country Albums chart for the last week of the year, even though an issue is not published. This chart is only available through *Billboard's* Web site or by mail. Our tabulations include this unpublished chart data.

1/11/64 - 14
Ring Of Fire (The Best Of Johnny Cash)...*Johnny Cash*

1/18/64 - 1
Night Life...*Ray Price*

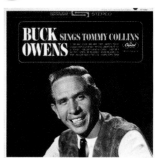

1/25/64 - 2
Buck Owens Sings Tommy Collins...
Buck Owens

5/9/64 - 6
Guitar Country...*Chet Atkins*

6/20/64 - 2
More Hank Snow Souvenirs...
Hank Snow

7/4/64 - 8
Moonlight and Roses...
Jim Reeves

8/29/64 - 4
I Walk The Line...*Johnny Cash*

9/26/64 - 8
The Best Of Jim Reeves...
Jim Reeves

11/21/64 - 7
Together Again/My Heart Skips A Beat...*Buck Owens And His Buckaroos*

1/9/65 - 13
I Don't Care...
Buck Owens And His Buckaroos

4/10/65 - 15
I've Got A Tiger By The Tail...
Buck Owens And His Buckaroos

7/10/65 - 7
Connie Smith...*Connie Smith*

8/14/65 - 2
The Easy Way...*Eddy Arnold*

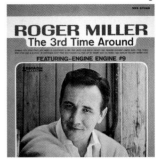

9/25/65 - 2
The 3rd Time Around...
Roger Miller

10/9/65 - 1
Before You Go/No One But You...
Buck Owens and his Buckaroos

10/16/65 - 2
Up Through The Years...
Jim Reeves

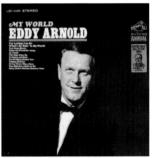

10/30/65 - 17
My World...*Eddy Arnold*

11/13/65 - 2
The First Thing Ev'ry Morning...
Jimmy Dean

12/25/65 - 2
Cute 'n' Country...
Connie Smith

3/26/66 - 2
Ballads of the Green Berets...
SSgt Barry Sadler

**4/9/66 - 8 — Roll out the red carpet
for Buck Owens and his
Buckaroos**...*Buck Owens*

4/23/66 - 2
I Want To Go With You...
Eddy Arnold

6/18/66 - 7
Distant Drums...*Jim Reeves*

8/6/66 - 2
I'm A People...*George Jones*

8/20/66 - 2
Dust On Mother's Bible...
Buck Owens And His Buckaroos

9/3/66 - 1
The Last Word In Lonesome...
Eddy Arnold

9/10/66 - 5
Carnegie Hall Concert...
Buck Owens And His Buckaroos

10/8/66 - 1
Almost Persuaded...
David Houston

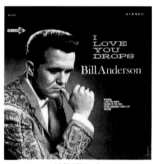

10/15/66 - 2
I Love You Drops...
Bill Anderson

11/5/66 - 2
Another Bridge To Burn...
Ray Price

11/12/66 - 2
You Ain't Woman Enough...
Loretta Lynn

12/3/66 - 1
Born To Sing...*Connie Smith*

12/10/66 - 2
**Swinging Doors and The Bottle Let
Me Down**...*Merle Haggard*

12/24/66 - 5
The Best Of Sonny James...
Sonny James

1/21/67 - 2
Somebody Like Me...*Eddy Arnold*

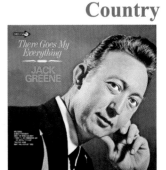

2/11/67 - 9
There Goes My Everything...
Jack Greene

3/18/67 - 1
Open Up Your Heart...
Buck Owens And His Buckaroos

4/15/67 - 3
Lonely Again...*Eddy Arnold*

4/29/67 - 1
Touch My Heart...*Ray Price*

**5/20/67 - 1 — Don't Come Home
A'Drinkin' (With Lovin' On Your
Mind)**...*Loretta Lynn*

5/27/67 - 7
The Best Of Eddy Arnold...
Eddy Arnold

7/15/67 - 1
Need You...*Sonny James
and the Southern Gentlemen*

**7/22/67 - 1 — Buck Owens And His
Buckaroos In Japan!**...*Buck Owens
And His Buckaroos*

7/29/67 - 5
All The Time...*Jack Greene*

8/26/67 - 2
It's Such A Pretty World Today...
Wynn Stewart

9/16/67 - 3
Johnny Cash's Greatest Hits, Volume 1...*Johnny Cash*

10/7/67 - 3
Ode To Billie Joe...
Bobbie Gentry

10/28/67 - 1
Your Tender Loving Care...
Buck Owens And His Buckaroos

11/4/67 - 13
Turn The World Around...
Eddy Arnold

12/16/67 - 1
Branded Man...
Merle Haggard And The Strangers

2/10/68 - 4
By The Time I Get To Phoenix...
Glen Campbell

3/9/68 - 1
Sing Me Back Home...
Merle Haggard And The Strangers

3/16/68 - 4 — **It Takes People Like You To Make People Like Me**...
Buck Owens And His Buckaroos

4/6/68 - 4
The Everlovin' World Of Eddy Arnold...*Eddy Arnold*

5/11/68 - 1
Promises, Promises...
Lynn Anderson

5/18/68 - 1
The Country Way...
Charley Pride

5/25/68 - 5
Honey...*Bobby Goldsboro*

6/8/68 - 1
Hey, Little One...
Glen Campbell

6/15/68 - 2
Fist City...*Loretta Lynn*

7/20/68 - 4
Johnny Cash At Folsom Prison...
Johnny Cash

8/10/68 - 6
A New Place In The Sun...
Glen Campbell

9/21/68 - 2
D-I-V-O-R-C-E...*Tammy Wynette*

10/12/68 - 2
Gentle On My Mind...
Glen Campbell

10/26/68 - 1
Bobbie Gentry & Glen Campbell...
Bobbie Gentry & Glen Campbell

11/2/68 - 4
Harper Valley P.T.A....
Jeannie C. Riley

11/30/68 - 20
Wichita Lineman...
Glen Campbell

4/19/69 - 11
Galveston...*Glen Campbell*

7/5/69 - 2
Songs My Father Left Me...
Hank Williams, Jr.

7/19/69 - 2
Same Train, A Different Time...
Merle Haggard

8/2/69 - 20
Johnny Cash At San Quentin...
Johnny Cash

12/20/69 - 13
The Best Of Charley Pride...
Charley Pride

1970

3/21/70 - 5
Okie From Muskogee...
Merle Haggard

3/28/70 - 4
Hello, I'm Johnny Cash...
Johnny Cash

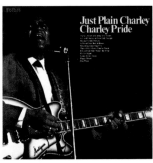

4/25/70 - 9
Just Plain Charley...
Charley Pride

7/25/70 - 2
Tammy's Touch...*Tammy Wynette*

8/8/70 - 8
Charley Pride's 10th Album...
Charley Pride

10/3/70 - 1
Hello Darlin'...*Conway Twitty*

10/10/70 - 7
The Fightin' Side Of Me...
Merle Haggard

1971

11/28/70 - 9
For The Good Times...*Ray Price*

12/19/70 - 2
The Johnny Cash Show...
Johnny Cash

2/13/71 - 14
Rose Garden...*Lynn Anderson*

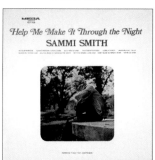

5/8/71 - 1
Help Me Make It Through The
Night...*Sammi Smith*

5/22/71 - 4
Hag...
Merle Haggard And The Strangers

6/26/71 - 1
Did You Think To Pray...
Charley Pride

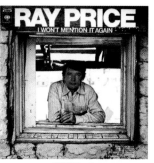

7/3/71 - 5
I Won't Mention It Again...
Ray Price

7/24/71 - 2
Man In Black...*Johnny Cash*

8/14/71 - 3
I'm Just Me...*Charley Pride*

8/28/71 - 7
You're My Man...*Lynn Anderson*

10/30/71 - 9
Easy Loving...*Freddie Hart*

1/1/72 - 16
Charley Pride Sings Heart Songs...
Charley Pride

4/22/72 - 16
**The Best Of Charley Pride,
Volume 2**...*Charley Pride*

8/12/72 - 4
**The Happiest Girl In The Whole
U.S.A.**....*Donna Fargo*

9/9/72 - 1
To Get To You...*Jerry Wallace*

9/16/72 - 10
**A Sunshiny Day with Charley
Pride**...*Charley Pride*

11/25/72 - 7
**The Best Of The Best Of Merle
Haggard**...*Merle Haggard*

1/13/73 - 2
Got The All Overs For You...
Freddie Hart And The Heartbeats

1/27/73 - 3
It's Not Love (But It's Not Bad)...
Merle Haggard And The Strangers

2/17/73 - 4
Songs of Love by Charley Pride...
Charley Pride

3/17/73 - 4
Dueling Banjos...
"Deliverance" Soundtrack

4/14/73 - 4
Aloha from Hawaii via Satellite...
Elvis Presley

5/12/73 - 1
My Second Album...*Donna Fargo*

5/19/73 - 1
Super Kind Of Woman...
Freddie Hart and The Heartbeats

5/26/73 - 1
Introducing Johnny Rodriguez...
Johnny Rodriguez

6/2/73 - 1
Entertainer Of The Year-Loretta...
Loretta Lynn

6/9/73 - 1
**The Rhymer And Other Five And
Dimers...***Tom T. Hall*

6/16/73 - 21
Behind Closed Doors...
Charlie Rich

7/7/73 - 1
Good Time Charlie...
Charlie McCoy

7/21/73 - 8
Satin Sheets...*Jeanne Pruett*

9/15/73 - 1
**Louisiana Woman-Mississippi
Man...***Conway Twitty - Loretta Lynn*

**9/22/73 - 2 — I Love Dixie Blues...so
I recorded "Live" in New Orleans...**
Merle Haggard and The Strangers

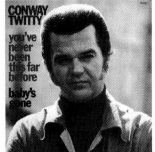

**10/6/73 - 3 — You've Never Been
This Far Before/Baby's Gone...**
Conway Twitty

10/27/73 - 1
Love Is The Foundation...
Loretta Lynn

11/3/73 - 1
Jesus Was A Capricorn...
Kris Kristofferson

11/10/73 - 1
Full Moon...
Kris Kristofferson & Rita Coolidge

11/17/73 - 3
Paper Roses...*Marie Osmond*

12/8/73 - 1
Primrose Lane/Don't Give Up On Me...*Jerry Wallace*

1974

2/16/74 - 2
Amazing Love...*Charley Pride*

3/2/74 - 2
Let Me Be There...
Olivia Newton-John

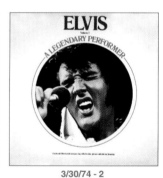

3/30/74 - 2
Elvis-A Legendary Performer,
Volume 1...*Elvis Presley*

4/13/74 - 2
There Won't Be Anymore...
Charlie Rich

4/27/74 - 5
Very Special Love Songs...
Charlie Rich

6/1/74 - 1
Conway Twitty's Honky Tonk
Angel...*Conway Twitty*

7/13/74 - 8
If You Love Me, Let Me Know...
Olivia Newton-John

8/24/74 - 13
Back Home Again...*John Denver*

9/21/74 - 1
Country Partners...
Loretta Lynn Conway Twitty

11/9/74 - 1
Room Full Of Roses...
Mickey Gilley

11/30/74 - 2
Merle Haggard Presents His 30th
Album...*Merle Haggard/The Strangers*

1975

1/11/75 - 1
The Silver Fox...*Charlie Rich*

1/18/75 - 2
I Can Help...*Billy Swan*

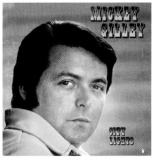

2/1/75 - 1
City Lights...*Mickey Gilley*

2/8/75 - 4
Heart Like A Wheel...
Linda Ronstadt

3/8/75 - 1
Promised Land...*Elvis Presley*

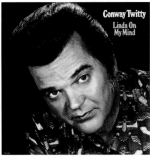

3/15/75 - 1
Linda On My Mind...
Conway Twitty

3/22/75 - 6
Have You Never Been Mellow...
Olivia Newton-John

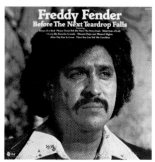

5/3/75 - 2
An Evening With John Denver...
John Denver

5/17/75 - 9
Before The Next Teardrop Falls...
Freddy Fender

6/14/75 - 4
Keep Movin' On...
Merle Haggard and The Strangers

8/16/75 - 1
Feelins'...
Loretta Lynn Conway Twitty

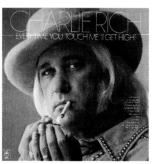

8/23/75 - 2
Every Time You Touch Me (I Get High)... Charlie Rich

9/6/75 - 1
Dreaming My Dreams...
Waylon Jennings

9/13/75 - 3
Rhinestone Cowboy...
Glen Campbell

10/4/75 - 5
Red Headed Stranger...
Willie Nelson

10/25/75 - 5
Windsong...*John Denver*

12/13/75 - 2
Are You Ready For Freddy...
Freddy Fender

12/27/75 - 9
Black Bear Road...*C.W. McCall*

1976

2/28/76 - 6 — The Outlaws...
*Waylon Jennings, Willie Nelson,
Jessi Colter, Tompall Glaser*

4/10/76 - 2
Elite Hotel...*Emmylou Harris*

4/24/76 - 8
The Sound In Your Mind...
Willie Nelson

5/1/76 - 1
It's All In The Movies...
Merle Haggard

6/26/76 - 2
Harmony...*Don Williams*

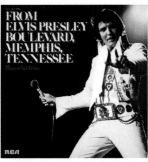

**7/10/76 - 4 — From Elvis Presley
Boulevard, Memphis, Tennessee**...
Elvis Presley

8/7/76 - 1
United Talent...
Loretta Lynn Conway Twitty

8/14/76 - 10
Are You Ready For The Country...
Waylon Jennings

8/28/76 - 1
Teddy Bear...*Red Sovine*

10/2/76 - 3
Hasten Down The Wind...
Linda Ronstadt

10/30/76 - 1
Golden Ring...
George Jones & Tammy Wynette

11/6/76 - 1
Here's Some Love...
Tanya Tucker

11/13/76 - 1
El Paso City...*Marty Robbins*

11/20/76 - 3
The Troublemaker...
Willie Nelson

12/11/76 - 1
Somebody Somewhere...
Loretta Lynn

1977

1/8/77 - 1
Conway Twitty's Greatest Hits
Vol. II...*Conway Twitty*

1/15/77 - 6
Waylon Live...*Waylon Jennings*

2/26/77 - 8
Luxury Liner...*Emmylou Harris*

4/23/77 - 3
Southern Nights...
Glen Campbell

5/14/77 - 1
New Harvest...First Gathering...
Dolly Parton

5/21/77 - 2
Kenny Rogers...*Kenny Rogers*

6/4/77 - 13
Ol' Waylon...*Waylon Jennings*

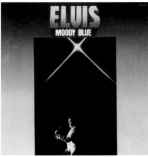

9/3/77 - 10
Moody Blue...*Elvis Presley*

11/12/77 - 5
Elvis In Concert...
Elvis Presley

12/17/77 - 1
Simple Dreams...*Linda Ronstadt*

12/24/77 - 9
Here You Come Again...
Dolly Parton

1978

2/25/78 - 11
Waylon & Willie...
Waylon Jennings & Willie Nelson

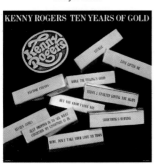

4/15/78 - 2
Ten Years Of Gold...
Kenny Rogers

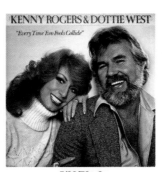

5/20/78 - 2
Every Time Two Fools Collide...
Kenny Rogers & Dottie West

6/10/78 - 11
Stardust...*Willie Nelson*

8/26/78 - 2
Love Or Something Like It...
Kenny Rogers

9/9/78 - 9
Heartbreaker...*Dolly Parton*

11/11/78 - 8
I've Always Been Crazy...
Waylon Jennings

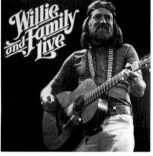

1/6/79 - 2
Willie and Family Live...
Willie Nelson

1/20/79 - 23
The Gambler...*Kenny Rogers*

6/2/79 - 16
Greatest Hits...
Waylon Jennings

9/1/79 - 4
Million Mile Reflections...
The Charlie Daniels Band

11/10/79 - 25
Kenny...*Kenny Rogers*

5/3/80 - 2
There's A Little Bit Of Hank In Me...
Charley Pride

5/10/80 - 7
Gideon...*Kenny Rogers*

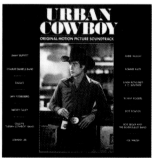

7/12/80 - 3
Music Man...*Waylon Jennings*

8/2/80 - 8
Urban Cowboy...
Soundtrack

9/13/80 - 2
Horizon...*Eddie Rabbitt*

10/4/80 - 6
Honeysuckle Rose...
Willie Nelson & Family/Soundtrack

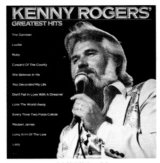

11/15/80 - 11
Kenny Rogers' Greatest Hits...
Kenny Rogers

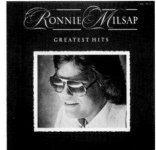

12/20/80 - 2
Greatest Hits...*Ronnie Milsap*

1981

2/14/81 - 10
9 To 5 And Odd Jobs...
Dolly Parton

5/2/81 - 3
Somewhere Over The Rainbow...
Willie Nelson

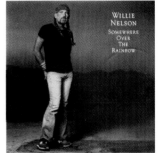

5/23/81 - 28
Feels So Right...*Alabama*

6/6/81 - 2
Seven Year Ache...*Rosanne Cash*

7/18/81 - 2
Fancy Free...*Oak Ridge Boys*

8/29/81 - 2
Share Your Love...*Kenny Rogers*

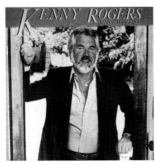

9/26/81 - 3
Step By Step...*Eddie Rabbitt*

10/17/81 - 3
There's No Gettin' Over Me...
Ronnie Milsap

141

1981—1984

12/5/81 - 4 — **Willie Nelson's Greatest Hits (& Some That Will Be)**...*Willie Nelson*

3/27/82 - 3
Bobbie Sue...*Oak Ridge Boys*

4/17/82 - 28
Mountain Music...*Alabama*

5/22/82 - 22
Always On My Mind...
Willie Nelson

11/20/82 - 1
Highways & Heartaches...
Ricky Skaggs

4/9/83 - 8
Pancho & Lefty...
Merle Haggard/Willie Nelson

4/16/83 - 21
The Closer You Get......
Alabama

10/29/83 - 16
Eyes That See In The Dark...
Kenny Rogers

2/18/84 - 5
Right Or Wrong...*George Strait*

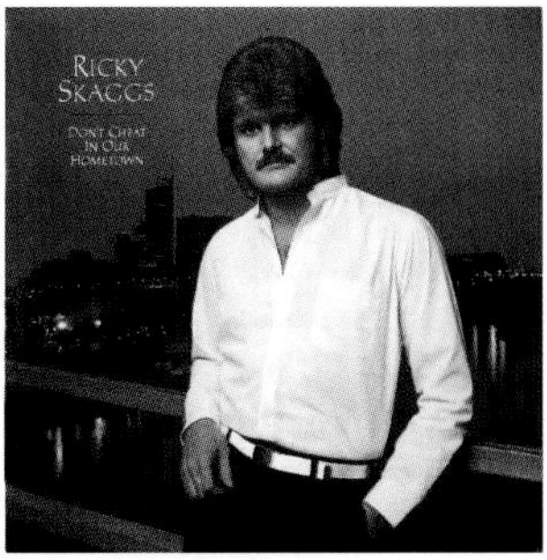

2/25/84 - 1
Don't Cheat In Our Hometown...
Ricky Skaggs

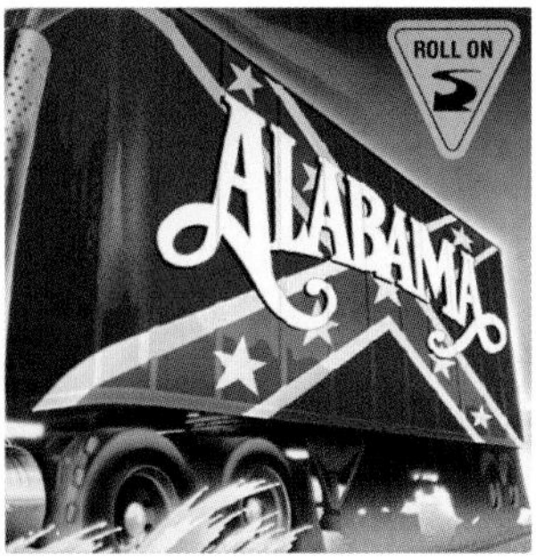

3/17/84 - 13
Roll On...*Alabama*

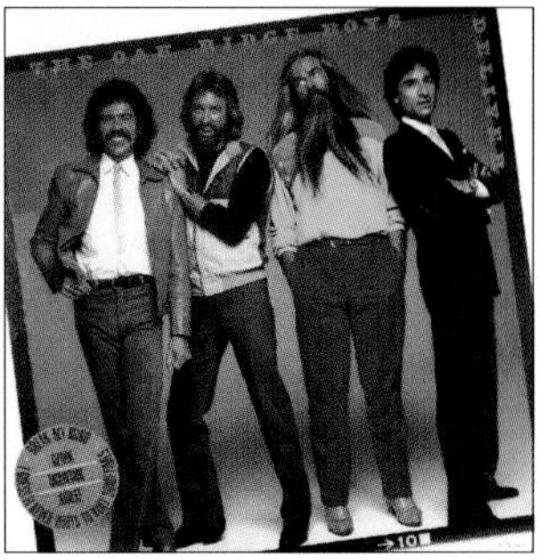

4/28/84 - 5
Deliver...*Oak Ridge Boys*

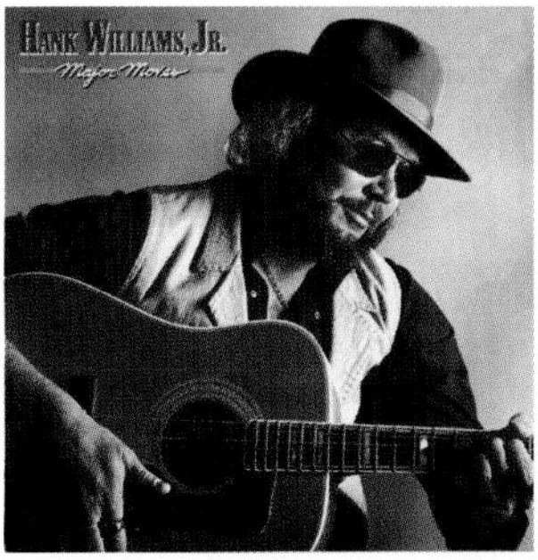

7/21/84 - 7
Major Moves...
Hank Williams, Jr.

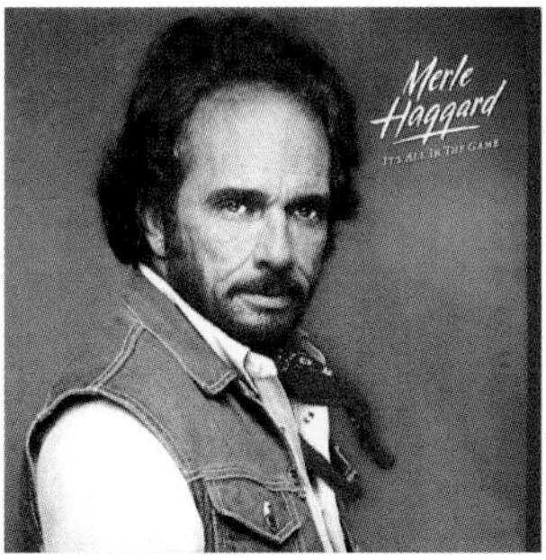

9/22/84 - 1
It's All In The Game...
Merle Haggard

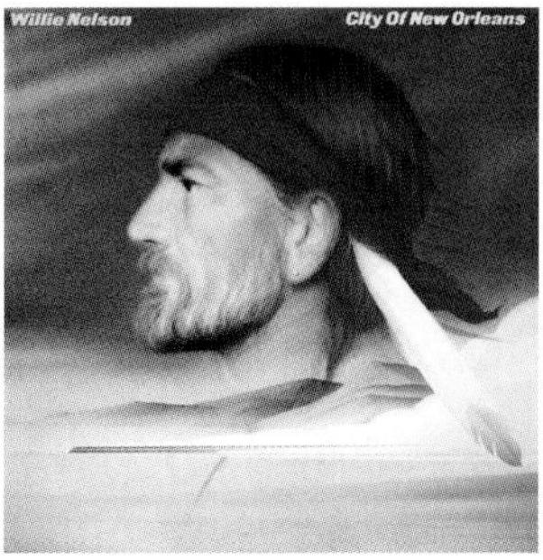

9/29/84 - 12
City Of New Orleans...
Willie Nelson

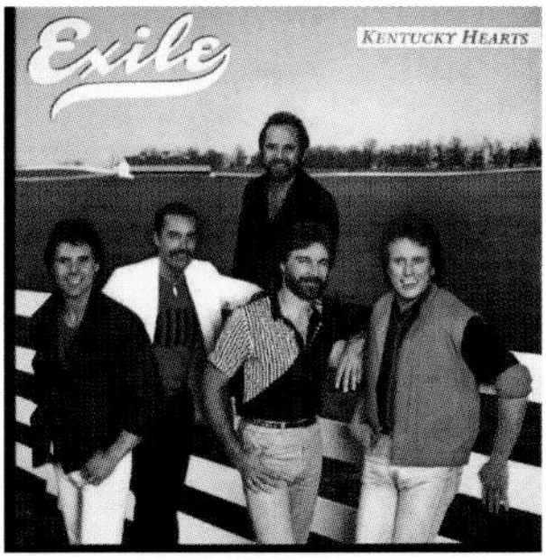

12/22/84 - 4
Kentucky Hearts...*Exile*

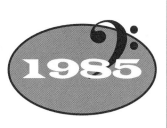

1985

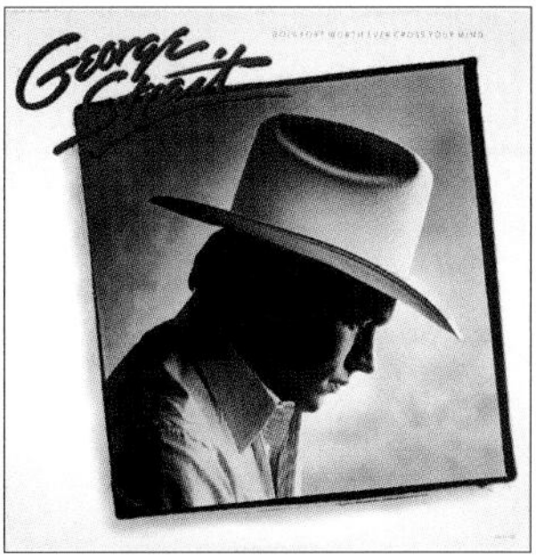

1/19/85 - 3
Does Fort Worth Ever Cross Your Mind...*George Strait*

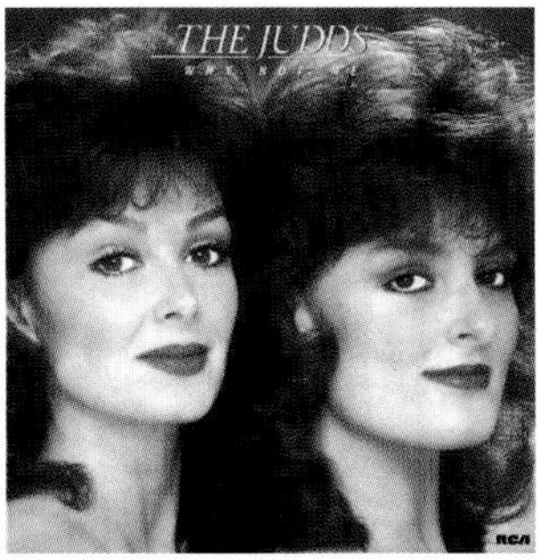

2/2/85 - 3
Why Not Me...*The Judds*

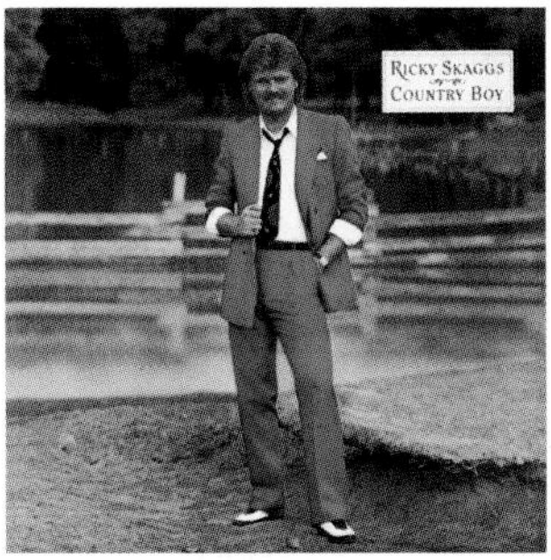

2/23/85 - 3
Country Boy...*Ricky Skaggs*

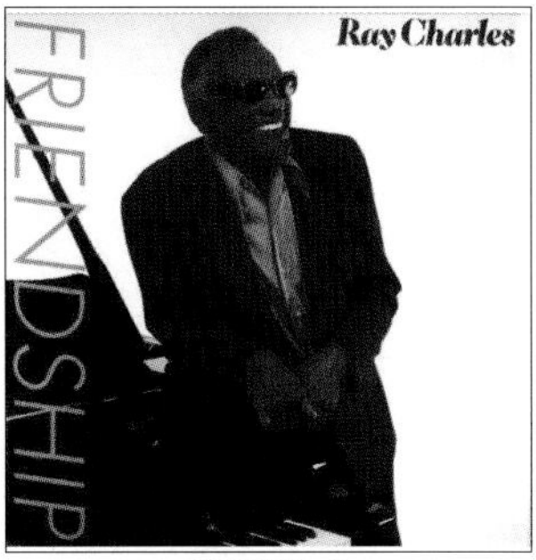

3/23/85 - 1
Friendship...*Ray Charles*

3/30/85 - 14
40 Hour Week...*Alabama*

6/22/85 - 10
Five-O...*Hank Williams, Jr.*

9/7/85 - 11
Greatest Hits, Vol. 2...
Ronnie Milsap

9/28/85 - 1 — **Highwayman**...
*Waylon Jennings/Willie Nelson/Johnny
Cash/Kris Kristofferson*

10/19/85 - 1
Pardners in Rhyme...
The Statler Brothers

12/7/85 - 1
Rhythm & Romance...
Rosanne Cash

12/14/85 - 1
Something Special...
George Strait

12/21/85 - 1
Anything Goes......*Gary Morris*

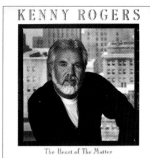

12/28/85 - 6
The Heart Of The Matter...
Kenny Rogers

2/8/86 - 2
Greatest Hits - Volume 2...
Hank Williams, Jr.

2/22/86 - 1
Streamline...*Lee Greenwood*

3/1/86 - 1
Rockin' With The Rhythm...
The Judds

3/8/86 - 1
Won't Be Blue Anymore...
Dan Seals

3/15/86 - 1
I Have Returned...*Ray Stevens*

3/22/86 - 1
Greatest Hits...
Earl Thomas Conley

3/29/86 - 1
Live In London...*Ricky Skaggs*

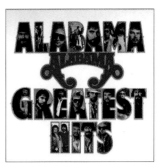

4/5/86 - 5
Greatest Hits...*Alabama*

4/19/86 - 1
A Memory Like You...
John Schneider

5/24/86 - 1
Whoever's In New England...
Reba McEntire

5/31/86 - 2
The Promiseland...
Willie Nelson

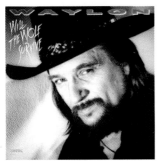

6/14/86 - 1
Will The Wolf Survive...
Waylon Jennings

6/21/86 - 1
Lost In The Fifties Tonight...
Ronnie Milsap

6/28/86 - 2
Guitars, Cadillacs, Etc., Etc....
Dwight Yoakam

7/12/86 - 4
#7...*George Strait*

8/9/86 - 8
Storms Of Life...*Randy Travis*

9/6/86 - 4
Montana Cafe...
Hank Williams, Jr.

10/4/86 - 1
Black & White...*Janie Frickie*

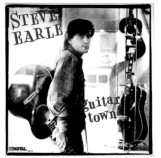

11/8/86 - 1
Guitar Town...*Steve Earle*

11/15/86 - 10
The Touch...*Alabama*

1/24/87 - 3
What Am I Gonna Do About You...
Reba McEntire

2/14/87 - 6
Ocean Front Property...
George Strait

3/21/87 - 3
Heartland...*The Judds*

4/11/87 - 1
Hank "Live"...
Hank Williams, Jr.

4/18/87 - 1
Wheels...*Restless Heart*

5/2/87 - 5
Trio...*Dolly Parton, Linda Ronstadt, Emmylou Harris*

6/6/87 - 2
Hillbilly Deluxe...
Dwight Yoakam

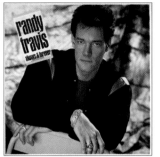

6/20/87 - 43
Always & Forever...
Randy Travis

8/29/87 - 1
Born To Boogie...
Hank Williams, Jr.

11/7/87 - 1
Greatest Hits, Volume Two...
George Strait

11/21/87 - 1
Just Us...*Alabama*

2/27/88 - 1
80's Ladies...*K.T. Oslin*

3/5/88 - 2
Wild-Eyed Dream...
Ricky Van Shelton

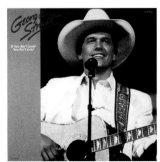

4/23/88 - 2
If You Ain't Lovin' You Ain't Livin'...
George Strait

6/11/88 - 8
Reba...*Reba McEntire*

8/6/88 - 1
Alabama Live...*Alabama*

147

8/13/88 - 2
Wild Streak...
Hank Williams, Jr.

8/27/88 - 16
Old 8x10...*Randy Travis*

10/22/88 - 1
Buenas Noches From A Lonely
Room...*Dwight Yoakam*

10/29/88 - 1
Greatest Hits...*The Judds*

11/5/88 - 10
Loving Proof...
Ricky Van Shelton

3/11/89 - 3
Southern Star...*Alabama*

4/1/89 - 11
Greatest Hits III...
Hank Williams, Jr.

4/29/89 - 1
Beyond The Blue Neon...
George Strait

6/24/89 - 13
Sweet Sixteen...*Reba McEntire*

9/23/89 - 31
Killin' Time...*Clint Black*

11/4/89 - 12
No Holdin' Back...*Randy Travis*

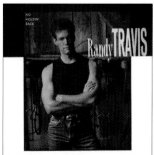

148

1990

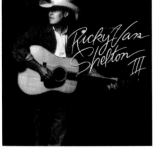

3/3/90 - 9
RVS III...*Ricky Van Shelton*

7/14/90 - 3
Livin' It Up...*George Strait*

10/13/90 - 41
No Fences...*Garth Brooks*

11/24/90 - 1
Heroes And Friends...
Randy Travis

12/22/90 - 7
Put Yourself In My Shoes...
Clint Black

1991

5/18/91 - 1
Eagle When She Flies...
Dolly Parton

9/28/91 - 33
Ropin' The Wind...*Garth Brooks*

1992

4/18/92 - 3
Wynonna...*Wynonna*

6/6/92 - 34
Some Gave All...
Billy Ray Cyrus

Country   1992 – 1994

10/10/92 - 16
The Chase...*Garth Brooks*

5/22/93 - 1
It's Your Call...*Reba McEntire*

5/29/93 - 5
Tell Me Why...*Wynonna*

7/3/93 - 1
Pure Country...
George Strait/Soundtrack

7/10/93 - 5
It Won't Be The Last...
Billy Ray Cyrus

8/14/93 - 5
**A Lot About Livin' (And A Little
'Bout Love)**...*Alan Jackson*

9/18/93 - 7
In Pieces...*Garth Brooks*

11/6/93 - 13
**Common Thread: The Songs Of The
Eagles**...*Various Artists*

1/22/94 - 1
Greatest Hits Volume Two...
Reba McEntire

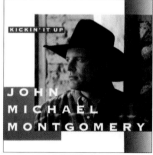

2/12/94 - 6
Kickin' It Up...
John Michael Montgomery

3/26/94 - 2
Rhythm Country And Blues...
Various Artists

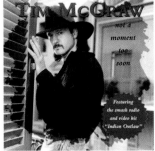

4/9/94 - 29
Not A Moment Too Soon...
Tim McGraw

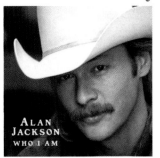

7/23/94 - 1
Who I Am...*Alan Jackson*

10/15/94 - 1
Waitin' On Sundown...
Brooks & Dunn

10/22/94 - 5
Stones In The Road...
Mary Chapin Carpenter

11/26/94 - 2
Lead On...*George Strait*

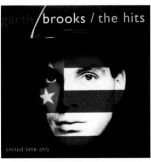

12/31/94 - 16
The Hits...*Garth Brooks*

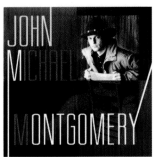

4/15/95 - 13
John Michael Montgomery...
John Michael Montgomery

7/22/95 - 29
The Woman In Me...*Shania Twain*

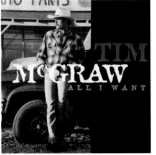

10/7/95 - 3
All I Want...*Tim McGraw*

10/21/95 - 2
Starting Over...*Reba McEntire*

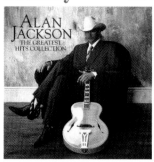

1996

11/11/95 - 4
The Greatest Hits Collection...
Alan Jackson

12/9/95 - 7
Fresh Horses... Garth Brooks

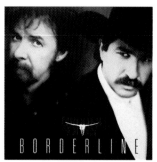

5/4/96 - 7
Borderline... Brooks & Dunn

5/11/96 - 1
Blue Clear Sky... George Strait

7/27/96 - 28
Blue... LeAnn Rimes

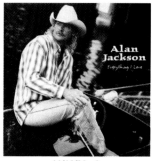

1997

11/16/96 - 3
Everything I Love...
Alan Jackson

11/30/96 - 1
What If It's You...
Reba McEntire

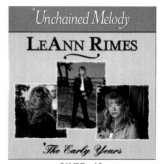

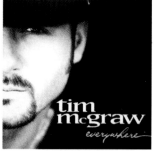

3/1/97 - 10
**Unchained Melody/The Early
Years...**LeAnn Rimes

5/10/97 - 6
Carrying Your Love With Me...
George Strait

6/21/97 - 11
Everywhere... Tim McGraw

9/13/97 - 2
Songbook - A Collection Of Hits...
Trisha Yearwood

9/27/97 - 9
You Light Up My Life - Inspirational
Songs...*LeAnn Rimes*

11/22/97 - 50
Come On Over...*Shania Twain*

12/13/97 - 13
Sevens...*Garth Brooks*

5/9/98 - 2
One Step At A Time...
George Strait

5/23/98 - 4
The Limited Series (boxed set)...
Garth Brooks

6/20/98 - 9
Hope Floats...*Soundtrack*

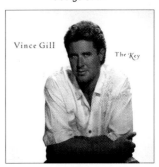

8/29/98 - 1
The Key...*Vince Gill*

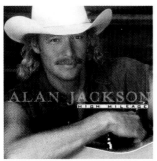

9/19/98 - 2
High Mileage...*Alan Jackson*

12/5/98 - 8
Double Live...*Garth Brooks*

1/30/99 - 7
Wide Open Spaces...
Dixie Chicks

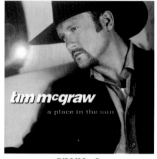

5/22/99 - 2
A Place In The Sun...
Tim McGraw

9/18/99 - 36
Fly...*Dixie Chicks*

11/13/99 - 2
LeAnn Rimes...*LeAnn Rimes*

11/27/99 - 6
Breathe...*Faith Hill*

12/18/99 - 1
Garth Brooks & The Magic Of Christmas...*Garth Brooks*

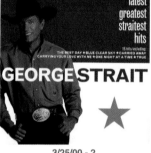

3/25/00 - 2
Latest Greatest Straitest Hits...
George Strait

6/10/00 - 1
I Hope You Dance...
Lee Ann Womack

8/19/00 - 1
Burn...*Jo Dee Messina*

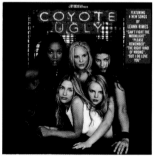

8/26/00 - 8
Coyote Ugly...*Soundtrack*

10/7/00 - 1
George Strait...*George Strait*

10/14/00 - 2
Greatest Hits...*Kenny Chesney*

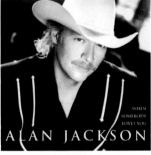

11/25/00 - 2
When Somebody Loves You...
Alan Jackson

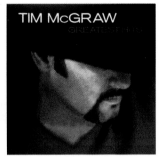

12/9/00 - 9
Greatest Hits...*Tim McGraw*

2/17/01 - 1
I Need You...*LeAnn Rimes*

2/24/01 - 35
O Brother, Where Art Thou?...
Soundtrack

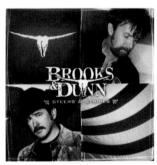

5/5/01 - 1
Steers & Stripes...
Brooks & Dunn

5/12/01 - 6
Set This Circus Down...
Tim McGraw

6/23/01 - 1
Inside Out...*Trisha Yearwood*

7/14/01 - 1
I'm Already There...*Lonestar*

9/15/01 - 1
Pull My Chain...*Toby Keith*

10/6/01 - 3
Greatest Hits...
Martina McBride

11/10/01 - 1
Greatest Hits Volume III - I'm A Survivor...*Reba McEntire*

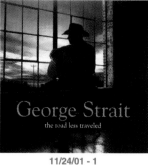

11/24/01 - 1
The Road Less Traveled...
George Strait

12/1/01 - 7
Scarecrow...*Garth Brooks*

2002

2/2/02 - 6
Drive...*Alan Jackson*

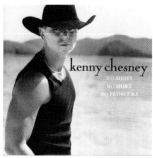

5/11/02 - 11
No Shoes, No Shirt, No Problems...
Kenny Chesney

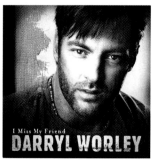

8/3/02 - 1
I Miss My Friend...
Darryl Worley

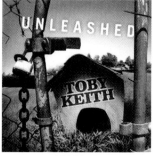

8/10/02 - 7
Unleashed...*Toby Keith*

9/14/02 - 19
Home...*Dixie Chicks*

10/12/02 - 3
Elv1s: 30 #1 Hits...
Elvis Presley

11/2/02 - 3
Cry...*Faith Hill*

11/16/02 - 1
Melt...*Rascal Flatts*

2003

12/7/02 - 6
Up!...*Shania Twain*

4/19/03 - 1
Chris Cagle...*Chris Cagle*

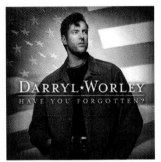

5/3/03 - 4
Have You Forgotten?...
Darryl Worley

6/7/03 - 1
Greatest Hits...*Jo Dee Messina*

6/21/03 - 2
From There To Here: Greatest Hits...
Lonestar

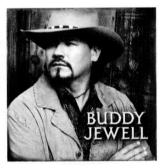

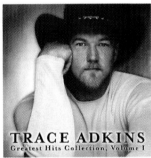

6/28/03 - 2
Honkytonkville...*George Strait*

7/19/03 - 1
Buddy Jewell...*Buddy Jewell*

7/26/03 - 1
Greatest Hits Collection, Volume I...
Trace Adkins

8/2/03 - 1
Red Dirt Road...*Brooks & Dunn*

8/9/03 - 2
Mud On The Tires...
Brad Paisley

8/23/03 - 1
**What The World Needs Now Is
Love**...*Wynonna*

2003 / 2004

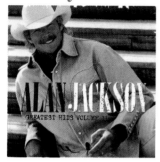

8/30/03 - 11
Greatest Hits Volume II and Some Other Stuff...*Alan Jackson*

10/18/03 - 1
Martina...*Martina McBride*

11/22/03 - 13
Shock'n Y'all...*Toby Keith*

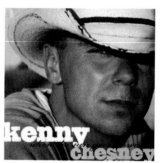

2/21/04 - 4+
When The Sun Goes Down...
Kenny Chesney

The All-Time #1 Country Albums

❶ **Come On Over**...*Shania Twain*
50 weeks at #1 — Year: 1997

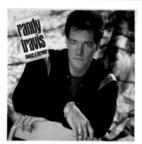

❷ **Always & Forever**...*Randy Travis*
43 weeks at #1 — Year: 1987

❸ **No Fences**...*Garth Brooks*
41 weeks at #1 — Year: 1990

❹ **Fly**...*Dixie Chicks*
36 weeks at #1 — Year: 1999

❺ **O Brother, Where Art Thou?**...*Soundtrack*
35 weeks at #1 — Year: 2001

❻ **Some Gave All**...*Billy Ray Cyrus*
34 weeks at #1 — Year: 1992

The Greatest #1s

#1 Pop Album
1945-1954

South Pacific...*Original Cast*
69 weeks at #1 — Year: 1949

#1 Pop Album
1955-2003

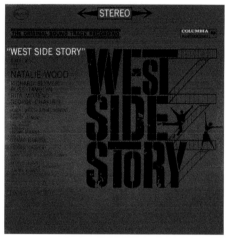

West Side Story...*Soundtrack*
54 weeks at #1 — Year: 1962

#1 R&B Album

Thriller...*Michael Jackson*
37 weeks at #1 — Year: 1983

#1 Country Album

Come On Over...*Shania Twain*
50 weeks at #1 — Year: 1997

THE ARTISTS

↓: repeat of album above arrow

A

AALIYAH
Pop 9/15/01 Aaliyah
R&B 12/28/02 I Care 4 U

ABDUL, Paula
Pop 10/7/89 Forever Your Girl
Pop 6/8/91 Spellbound

AC/DC
Pop 12/26/81 For Those About To
Rock We Salute You

ACE OF BASE
Pop 4/2/94 The Sign

ADAMS, Bryan
Pop 8/10/85 Reckless

ADDERLEY, "Cannonball", Quintet
R&B 4/1/67 Mercy, Mercy, Mercy!

ADKINS, Trace
C&W 7/26/03 Greatest Hits
Collection, Volume I

AEROSMITH
Pop 5/8/93 Get A Grip
Pop 4/5/97 Nine Lives

AGUILERA, Christina
Pop 9/11/99 Christina Aguilera

AIKEN, Clay
Pop 11/1/03 Measure Of A Man

ALABAMA
C&W 5/23/81 Feels So Right
C&W 4/17/82 Mountain Music
C&W 4/16/83 The Closer You Get...
C&W 3/17/84 Roll On
C&W 3/30/85 40 Hour Week
C&W 4/5/86 Greatest Hits
C&W 11/15/86 The Touch
C&W 11/21/87 Just Us
C&W 8/6/88 Alabama Live
C&W 3/11/89 Southern Star

AL B. SURE!
R&B 7/2/88 In Effect Mode

ALICE IN CHAINS
Pop 2/12/94 Jar Of Flies
Pop 11/25/95 Alice In Chains

ALLMAN BROTHERS BAND, The
Pop 9/8/73 Brothers And Sisters

ALPERT, Herb, & The Tijuana Brass
Pop 11/27/65 Whipped Cream &
Other Delights
Pop 3/5/66 Going Places
Pop 5/28/66 What Now My Love
Pop 6/17/67 Sounds Like
Pop 7/27/68 The Beat Of The
Brass

AMERICA
Pop 3/25/72 America

ANDERSON, Bill
C&W 10/15/66 I Love You Drops

ANDERSON, Lynn
C&W 5/11/68 Promises, Promises
C&W 2/13/71 Rose Garden
C&W 8/28/71 You're My Man

ARMSTRONG, Louis
Pop 6/13/64 Hello, Dolly!

ARNOLD, Eddy
C&W 8/14/65 The Easy Way
C&W 10/30/65 My World
C&W 4/23/66 I Want To Go With You
C&W 9/3/66 The Last Word In
Lonesome
C&W 1/21/67 Somebody Like Me
C&W 4/15/67 Lonely Again
C&W 5/27/67 The Best Of Eddy
Arnold
C&W 11/4/67 Turn The World
Around
C&W 4/6/68 The Everlovin' World
Of Eddy Arnold

ASHANTI
Pop 4/20/02 Ashanti
R&B 4/20/02 ↓
Pop 7/19/03 Chapter II
R&B 7/19/03 ↓

ASHFORD & SIMPSON
R&B 10/21/78 Is It Still Good To Ya
R&B 2/9/85 Solid

ASIA
Pop 5/15/82 Asia

ATKINS, Chet
C&W 5/9/64 Guitar Country

ATLANTIC STARR
R&B 5/8/82 Brilliance

AVERAGE WHITE BAND
Pop 2/22/75 AWB
R&B 3/1/75 ↓
R&B 8/23/75 Cut The Cake

AZ
R&B 10/28/95 Doe Or Die

B

BABYFACE
R&B 10/14/89 Tender Lover

BACHMAN-TURNER OVERDRIVE
Pop 10/19/74 Not Fragile

BACKSTREET BOYS
Pop 6/5/99 Millennium
Pop 12/9/00 Black & Blue

BAD BOY'S DA BAND
R&B 10/18/03 Too Hot For T.V.

BAD COMPANY
Pop 9/28/74 Bad Company

BADU, Erykah
R&B 3/1/97 Baduizm
R&B 12/6/97 Live

BAKER, Anita
R&B 9/20/86 Rapture
R&B 11/19/88 Giving You The Best
That I Got
Pop 12/24/88 ↓
R&B 10/1/94 Rhythm Of Love

BAND, The — see DYLAN, Bob

BANNER, David
R&B 6/7/03 Mississippi: The
Album

BEACH BOYS, The
Pop 12/5/64 Beach Boys Concert
Pop 10/5/74 Endless Summer

BEASTIE BOYS
Pop 3/7/87 Licensed To Ill
Pop 6/18/94 Ill Communication
Pop 8/1/98 Hello Nasty

BEATLES, The
Pop 2/15/64 Meet The Beatles!
Pop 5/2/64 The Beatles' Second
Album
Pop 7/25/64 A Hard Day's Night
Pop 1/9/65 Beatles '65
Pop 7/10/65 Beatles VI
Pop 9/11/65 Help!
Pop 1/8/66 Rubber Soul
Pop 7/30/66 "Yesterday"...And
Today
Pop 9/10/66 Revolver
Pop 7/1/67 Sgt. Pepper's Lonely
Hearts Club Band
Pop 1/6/68 Magical Mystery Tour
Pop 12/28/68 The Beatles [White
Album]
Pop 11/1/69 Abbey Road
Pop 6/13/70 Let It Be
Pop 5/26/73 The Beatles/
1967-1970
Pop 12/9/95 Anthology 1
Pop 4/6/96 Anthology 2
Pop 11/16/96 Anthology 3
Pop 12/2/00 1

BEE GEES
Pop 1/21/78 Saturday Night Fever
R&B 2/18/78 ↓
Pop 3/3/79 Spirits Having Flown
Pop 1/12/80 Bee Gees Greatest

BELAFONTE, Harry
Pop 3/24/56 Belafonte
Pop 9/8/56 Calypso

BELL BIV DeVOE
R&B 6/2/90 Poison

BELLE, Regina
R&B 12/2/89 Stay With Me

BENATAR, Pat
Pop 8/15/81 Precious Time

BENSON, George
R&B 5/22/76 Breezin'
Pop 7/31/76 ↓
R&B 4/29/78 Weekend In L.A.
R&B 9/20/80 Give Me The Night

BEYONCÉ
Pop 7/12/03 Dangerously In Love
R&B 7/12/03 ↓

BIG BROTHER & THE HOLDING COMPANY
Pop 10/12/68 Cheap Thrills

BIG PUNISHER
R&B 5/16/98 Capital Punishment
R&B 4/22/00 Yeeeah Baby
       BIG PUN

BIG TYMERS
R&B 6/3/00 I Got That Work
Pop 5/18/02 Hood Rich
R&B 5/18/02 ↓

BLACK, Clint
C&W 9/23/89 Killin' Time
C&W 12/22/90 Put Yourself In My Shoes

BLACK CROWES, The
Pop 5/30/92 The Southern Harmony And Musical Companion

BLACK ROB
R&B 3/25/00 Life Story

BLACKstreet
R&B 10/5/96 Another Level

BLIGE, Mary J.
R&B 10/3/92 What's The 411?
R&B 12/17/94 My Life
Pop 5/10/97 Share My World
R&B 5/10/97 ↓
R&B 9/4/99 Mary
R&B 9/15/01 No More Drama
Pop 9/13/03 Love & Life
R&B 9/13/03 ↓

BLIND FAITH
Pop 9/20/69 Blind Faith

BLINK-182
Pop 6/30/01 Take Off Your Pants And Jacket

BLOOD, SWEAT & TEARS
Pop 3/29/69 Blood, Sweat & Tears
Pop 8/8/70 Blood, Sweat & Tears 3

BLUES BROTHERS
Pop 2/3/79 Briefcase Full Of Blues

BOLTON, Michael
Pop 5/25/91 Time, Love & Tenderness
Pop 11/21/92 Timeless (The Classics)

BONE CRUSHER
R&B 5/17/03 AttenCHUN!

BONE THUGS-N-HARMONY
Pop 8/12/95 E. 1999 Eternal
R&B 8/12/95 ↓
Pop 8/16/97 The Art Of War
R&B 8/16/97 ↓
R&B 3/18/00 BTNH-RESURRECTION

BON JOVI
Pop 10/25/86 Slippery When Wet
Pop 10/15/88 New Jersey

BOSTON
Pop 9/16/78 Don't Look Back
Pop 11/1/86 Third Stage

BOYZ II MEN
R&B 8/24/91 Cooleyhighharmony
Pop 9/17/94 II
R&B 9/17/94 ↓
Pop 10/11/97 Evolution
R&B 10/11/97 ↓

BRANDY
R&B 3/23/02 Full Moon

BRASS CONSTRUCTION
R&B 4/24/76 Brass Construction

BRAXTON, Toni
R&B 10/2/93 Toni Braxton
Pop 2/26/94 ↓
R&B 7/6/96 Secrets
R&B 5/13/00 The Heat

BRICK
R&B 1/8/77 Good High
R&B 11/12/77 Brick

BROOKS, Garth
C&W 10/13/90 No Fences
Pop 9/28/91 Ropin' The Wind
C&W 9/28/91 ↓
Pop 10/10/92 The Chase
C&W 10/10/92 ↓
Pop 9/18/93 In Pieces
C&W 9/18/93 ↓
C&W 12/31/94 The Hits
Pop 1/7/95 ↓
Pop 12/9/95 Fresh Horses
Pop 12/13/97 Sevens
C&W 12/13/97 ↓
Pop 5/23/98 The Limited Series
C&W 5/23/98 ↓
Pop 12/5/98 Double Live
C&W 12/5/98 ↓
C&W 12/18/99 Garth Brooks & The Magic Of Christmas
Pop 12/1/01 Scarecrow
C&W 12/1/01 ↓

BROOKS & DUNN
C&W 10/15/94 Waitin' On Sundown
C&W 5/4/96 Borderline
C&W 5/5/01 Steers & Stripes
C&W 8/2/03 Red Dirt Road

BROTHERS JOHNSON, The
R&B 5/29/76 Look Out For #1
R&B 9/2/78 Blam!!
R&B 4/19/80 Light Up The Night

BROWN, Bobby
R&B 9/10/88 Don't Be Cruel
Pop 1/21/89 ↓
R&B 11/7/92 Bobby

BROWN, Foxy
Pop 2/13/99 Chyna Doll
R&B 2/13/99 ↓

BROWN, James
R&B 5/4/74 The Payback

BROWNE, Jackson
Pop 9/13/80 Hold Out

BROWNE, Tom
R&B 10/18/80 Love Approach

BRYSON, Peabo
R&B 10/5/91 Can You Stop The Rain

B.T. EXPRESS
R&B 2/22/75 Do It ('Til You're Satisfied)
R&B 9/6/75 Non-Stop

B2K
R&B 3/30/02 B2K

BUSH
Pop 12/7/96 Razorblade Suitcase

BUSTA RHYMES
R&B 4/13/96 The Coming
R&B 10/4/97 When Disaster Strikes...
R&B 7/8/00 Anarchy

BYRD, Charlie — see GETZ, Stan

C

CAGLE, Chris
C&W 4/19/03 Chris Cagle

CAMEO
R&B 7/12/80 Cameosis
R&B 4/28/84 She's Strange
R&B 10/25/86 Word Up!

CAMPBELL, Glen
C&W 2/10/68 By The Time I Get To Phoenix
C&W 6/8/68 Hey, Little One
C&W 8/10/68 A New Place In The Sun
C&W 10/12/68 Gentle On My Mind
C&W 10/26/68 Bobbie Gentry & Glen Campbell
C&W 11/30/68 Wichita Lineman
Pop 12/21/68 ↓
C&W 4/19/69 Galveston
C&W 9/13/75 Rhinestone Cowboy
C&W 4/23/77 Southern Nights

CAM'RON
R&B 6/1/02 Come Home With Me

CAPPADONNA
R&B 4/11/98 The Pillage

CAREY, Mariah
Pop 3/2/91 Mariah Carey
R&B 9/18/93 Music Box
Pop 12/25/93 ↓
Pop 10/21/95 Daydream
R&B 10/21/95 ↓
Pop 10/4/97 Butterfly

CARLE, Frankie, and his Orchestra
Pop 1/29/49 Roses In Rhythm

CARLISLE, Bob
Pop 6/28/97 Butterfly Kisses (Shades Of Grace)

CARNES, Kim
Pop 6/27/81 Mistaken Identity

CARPENTER, Mary-Chapin
C&W 10/22/94 Stones In The Road

CARPENTERS
Pop 1/5/74 The Singles 1969-1973

CASH, Johnny

C&W	1/11/64	Ring Of Fire (The Best Of Johnny Cash)
C&W	8/29/64	I Walk The Line
C&W	9/16/67	Johnny Cash's Greatest Hits, Volume 1
C&W	7/20/68	Johnny Cash At Folsom Prison
C&W	8/2/69	Johnny Cash At San Quentin
Pop	8/23/69	↓
C&W	3/28/70	Hello, I'm Johnny Cash
C&W	12/19/70	The Johnny Cash Show
C&W	7/24/71	Man In Black
C&W	9/28/85	Highwayman

WILLIE NELSON/ JOHNNY CASH/ WAYLON JENNINGS/ KRIS KRISTOFFERSON

CASH, Rosanne

C&W	6/6/81	Seven Year Ache
C&W	12/7/85	Rhythm & Romance

CAVALLARO, Carmen, And His Orchestra

Pop	7/20/46	Dancing In The Dark
Pop	5/22/48	Song Hits of 1932

CHANGING FACES

R&B	9/10/94	Changing Faces

CHAPMAN, Tracy

Pop	8/27/88	Tracy Chapman

CHARLES, Ray

Pop	6/23/62	Modern Sounds In Country And Western Music
R&B	5/14/66	Crying Time
C&W	3/23/85	Friendship

CHESNEY, Kenny

C&W	10/14/00	Greatest Hits
Pop	5/11/02	No Shoes, No Shirt, No Problems
C&W	5/11/02	↓
Pop	2/21/04	When The Sun Goes Down
C&W	2/21/04	↓

CHIC

R&B	12/16/78	C'est Chic

CHICAGO

Pop	8/19/72	Chicago V
Pop	7/28/73	Chicago VI
Pop	4/27/74	Chicago VII
Pop	5/3/75	Chicago VIII
Pop	12/13/75	Chicago IX - Chicago's Greatest Hits

CHI-LITES, The

R&B	6/10/72	A Lonely Man

CLAPTON, Eric

Pop	8/17/74	461 Ocean Boulevard
Pop	3/13/93	Unplugged
Pop	10/1/94	From The Cradle

CLARKSON, Kelly

Pop	5/3/03	Thankful

CLIBURN, Van

Pop	8/11/58	Tchaikovsky: Piano Concerto No. 1

CLIPSE

R&B	9/7/02	Lord Willin'

C-MURDER

R&B	4/4/98	Life Or Death
R&B	3/27/99	Bossalinie
R&B	9/23/00	Trapped In Crime

COLE, Nat "King"

Pop	3/24/45	The King Cole Trio
Pop	8/17/46	King Cole Trio, Volume 2
Pop	5/27/57	Love Is The Thing

COLE, Natalie

R&B	11/22/75	Inseparable
R&B	4/2/77	Unpredictable
Pop	7/27/91	Unforgettable With Love

COLLINS, Phil

Pop	3/30/85	No Jacket Required
Pop	1/6/90	...But Seriously

COLLINS, William "Bootsy"

R&B	4/23/77	Ahh...The Name Is Bootsy, Baby!
R&B	3/25/78	Bootsy? Player Of The Year

COLTER, Jessi — see JENNINGS, Waylon

COMMODORES

R&B	8/28/76	Hot On The Tracks
R&B	5/21/77	Commodores
R&B	6/24/78	Natural High
R&B	9/15/79	Midnight Magic
R&B	4/6/85	Nightshift

COMO, Perry

Pop	11/16/46	Merry Christmas Music
Pop	2/28/48	A Sentimental Date With Perry

COMPTON'S MOST WANTED — see MC EIHT

CONLEY, Earl Thomas

C&W	3/22/86	Greatest Hits

COOKE, Sam

R&B	2/6/65	Sam Cooke At The Copa
R&B	2/27/65	Shake

COOLIDGE, Rita — see KRISTOFFERSON, Kris

COOPER, Alice

Pop	4/21/73	Billion Dollar Babies

COSBY, Bill

R&B	7/15/67	Revenge

COUNTING CROWS

Pop	11/2/96	Recovering The Satellites

CRAZY OTTO

Pop	5/28/55	Crazy Otto

CREAM

Pop	8/10/68	Wheels Of Fire

CREED

Pop	10/16/99	Human Clay
Pop	12/8/01	Weathered

CREEDENCE CLEARWATER REVIVAL

Pop	10/4/69	Green River
Pop	8/22/70	Cosmo's Factory

CROCE, Jim

Pop	1/12/74	You Don't Mess Around With Jim

CROSBY, Bing

Pop	10/20/45	Going My Way
Pop	12/8/45	Merry Christmas
Pop	3/23/46	The Bells Of St. Mary's
Pop	11/23/46	Merry Christmas
Pop	11/15/47	↓
Pop	3/20/48	St. Patrick's Day
Pop	11/20/48	Merry Christmas
Pop	12/24/49	↓
Pop	12/16/50	↓
Pop	12/30/57	↓

CROSBY, STILLS, NASH & YOUNG

Pop	5/16/70	Deja Vu
Pop	5/15/71	4 Way Street
Pop	11/2/74	So Far

CYPRESS HILL

Pop	8/7/93	Black Sunday
R&B	8/7/93	↓

CYRUS, Billy Ray

C&W	6/6/92	Some Gave All
Pop	6/13/92	↓
C&W	7/10/93	It Won't Be The Last

D

DA BRAT

R&B	7/30/94	Funkdafied
R&B	4/29/00	Unrestricted

D'ANGELO

Pop	2/12/00	Voodoo
R&B	2/12/00	↓

DANIELS, Charlie, Band

C&W	9/1/79	Million Mile Reflections

D'ARBY, Terence Trent

R&B	4/30/88	Introducing The Hardline According To Terence Trent D'Arby

DAS EFX

R&B	6/20/92	Dead Serious

DAVIS, Sammy Jr.

Pop	6/11/55	Starring Sammy Davis, Jr.

DAY, Doris

Pop	5/13/50	Young Man With A Horn

DORIS DAY and HARRY JAMES

Pop	4/21/51	Lullaby Of Broadway
Pop	3/15/52	I'll See You In My Dreams
Pop	7/23/55	Love Me Or Leave Me

DAZZ BAND

R&B	6/19/82	Keep It Live

DEAN, Jimmy

C&W	11/13/65	The First Thing Ev'ry Morning

DEF LEPPARD
Pop 7/23/88 Hysteria
Pop 4/18/92 Adrenalize

DEF SQUAD
R&B 7/18/98 El Niño

DE LA SOUL
R&B 5/27/89 3 Feet High And
             Rising

DENNY, Martin (The
Exciting Sounds Of)
Pop 6/22/59 Exotica

DENVER, John
Pop 3/30/74 John Denver's
             Greatest Hits
Pop 8/10/74 Back Home Again
C&W 8/24/74 ↓
C&W 5/3/75 An Evening With
             John Denver
Pop 10/18/75 Windsong
C&W 10/25/75 ↓

DEPECHE MODE
Pop 4/10/93 Songs Of Faith And
             Devotion

DESTINY'S CHILD
Pop 5/19/01 Survivor
R&B 5/19/01 ↓

DION, Celine
Pop 10/5/96 Falling Into You
Pop 1/17/98 Let's Talk About Love
Pop 12/11/99 All The Way...A
             Decade Of Song
Pop 4/13/02 A New Day Has
             Come

DIPLOMATS, The
R&B 4/12/03 Diplomatic Immunity

DIRE STRAITS
Pop 8/31/85 Brothers In Arms

DISTURBED
Pop 10/5/02 Believe

DISTURBING THA
PEACE
R&B 10/5/02 Golden Grain

DIXIE CHICKS
C&W 1/30/99 Wide Open Spaces
Pop 9/18/99 Fly
C&W 9/18/99 ↓
Pop 9/14/02 Home
C&W 9/14/02 ↓

DJ CLUE?
R&B 9/16/00 Backstage Mixtape
R&B 3/17/01 The Professional 2

DJ QUIK
R&B 3/11/95 Safe + Sound

DMX
Pop 6/6/98 It's Dark And Hell Is
             Hot
R&B 6/6/98 ↓
Pop 1/9/99 Flesh Of My Flesh
             Blood Of My Blood
R&B 1/9/99 ↓
Pop 1/8/00 ...And Then There
             Was X
R&B 1/8/00 ↓
Pop 11/10/01 The Great
             Depression
R&B 11/10/01 ↓

Pop 10/4/03 Grand Champ
R&B 10/4/03 ↓

D.O.C., The
R&B 9/30/89 No One Can Do It
             Better

DR. DRE
R&B 2/6/93 The Chronic
R&B 12/4/99 2001

DOGG POUND, Tha
Pop 11/18/95 Dogg Food
R&B 11/18/95 ↓

DOOBIE BROTHERS,
The
Pop 4/7/79 Minute By Minute

DOORS, The
Pop 9/7/68 Waiting For The Sun

DOUGLAS, Carl
R&B 2/8/75 Kung Fu Fighting And
             Other Great Love
             Songs

D12
Pop 7/7/01 Devil's Night
R&B 7/7/01 ↓

DUFF, Hilary
Pop 9/20/03 Metamorphosis

DUPRI, Jermaine
R&B 8/8/98 Jermaine Dupri
             Presents Life In
             1472 - The Original
             Soundtrack

DYLAN, Bob
Pop 2/16/74 Planet Waves
             BOB DYLAN With The
             Band
Pop 3/1/75 Blood On The Tracks
Pop 2/7/76 Desire

E

EAGLES
Pop 7/26/75 One Of These Nights
Pop 3/13/76 Eagles/Their Greatest
             Hits 1971-1975
Pop 1/15/77 Hotel California
Pop 11/3/79 The Long Run
Pop 11/26/94 Hell Freezes Over

EARLE, Steve
C&W 11/8/86 Guitar Town

EARTH, WIND & FIRE
R&B 5/25/74 Open Our Eyes
R&B 4/19/75 That's The Way Of
             The World
Pop 5/17/75 ↓
Pop 1/3/76 Gratitude
Pop 1/17/76 ↓
R&B 12/17/77 All 'N All
R&B 7/14/79 I Am
R&B 11/28/81 Raise!

EAZY-E
R&B 11/6/93 It's On (Dr. Dre)
             187um Killa
R&B 2/17/96 Str8 Off Tha Streetz
             Of Muthaphukkin
             Compton

EIGHTBALL & MJG
R&B 6/5/99 In Our Lifetime

ELLIOTT, Missy
"Misdemeanor"
R&B 8/2/97 Supa Dupa Fly
R&B 7/10/99 Da Real World
R&B 6/2/01 Miss E... So Addictive

EMINEM
R&B 4/10/99 The Slim Shady LP
Pop 6/10/00 The Marshall Mathers
             LP
R&B 6/10/00 ↓
Pop 6/8/02 The Eminem Show
R&B 6/8/02 ↓

EMOTIONS, The
R&B 7/23/77 Rejoice

EN VOGUE
R&B 5/9/92 Funky Divas

EPMD
R&B 8/20/88 Strictly Business
R&B 9/16/89 Unfinished Business
R&B 3/23/91 Business As Usual

EVE
Pop 10/2/99 Ruff Ryders' First
             Lady
R&B 10/2/99 ↓
R&B 3/24/01 Scorpion
R&B 9/14/02 Eve-olution

EXILE
C&W 12/22/84 Kentucky Hearts

F

FARGO, Donna
C&W 8/12/72 The Happiest Girl In
             The Whole U.S.A.
C&W 5/12/73 My Second Album

FENDER, Freddy
C&W 5/17/75 Before The Next
             Teardrop Falls
C&W 12/13/75 Are You Ready For
             Freddy

FIEND
R&B 5/23/98 There's One In Every
             Family
R&B 7/24/99 Street Life

50 CENT
Pop 2/22/03 Get Rich Or Die Tryin'
R&B 2/22/03 ↓
R&B 5/3/03 The New Breed

FINE YOUNG
CANNIBALS
Pop 6/3/89 The Raw & The
             Cooked

FIRM, The
Pop 11/8/97 The Firm - The Album
R&B 11/8/97 ↓

FISHER, Eddie
Pop 11/1/52 I'm In The Mood For
             Love
Pop 1/3/53 Christmas With Eddie
             Fisher

504 BOYZ
R&B 5/20/00 Goodfellas

FLACK, Roberta
Pop 4/29/72 First Take
R&B 5/27/72 ↓

FLANAGAN, Ralph, and his Orchestra

Pop 7/22/50 Ralph Flanagan plays Rodgers & Hammerstein II for dancing

FLEETWOOD MAC

Pop 9/4/76 Fleetwood Mac
Pop 4/2/77 Rumours
Pop 8/7/82 Mirage
Pop 9/6/97 The Dance

FLOATERS, The

R&B 8/6/77 The Floaters

FOGERTY, John

Pop 3/23/85 Centerfield

FONTAINE, Frank

Pop 3/16/63 Songs I Sing On The Jackie Gleason Show

FOREIGNER

Pop 8/22/81 4

FOUR TOPS

R&B 7/3/65 Four Tops
R&B 2/4/67 Four Tops Live!

FRAMPTON, Peter

Pop 4/10/76 Frampton Comes Alive!

FRANKLIN, Aretha

R&B 4/29/67 I Never Loved A Man The Way I Love You
R&B 9/9/67 Aretha Arrives
R&B 3/2/68 Aretha: Lady Soul
R&B 7/27/68 Aretha Now
R&B 3/1/69 Aretha Franklin: Soul '69
R&B 7/26/69 Aretha's Gold
R&B 6/19/71 Aretha Live At Fillmore West
R&B 5/18/74 Let Me In Your Life
R&B 7/31/76 Sparkle
R&B 9/4/82 Jump To It

FRANKLIN, Kirk

R&B 3/9/02 The Rebirth Of Kirk Franklin

FRICKE, Janie

C&W 10/4/86 Black & White

FROMAN, Jane

Pop 5/3/52 With A Song In My Heart...

FUGEES (REFUGEE CAMP)

R&B 3/23/96 The Score
Pop 5/25/96 ↓

FUNKADELIC

R&B 10/28/78 One Nation Under A Groove

G

GANG STARR

R&B 4/18/98 Moment Of Truth

GAP BAND, The

R&B 2/21/81 The Gap Band III
R&B 7/3/82 Gap Band IV
R&B 3/9/85 Gap Band VI

GARLAND, Judy

Pop 9/11/61 Judy At Carnegie Hall

GAYE, Marvin

R&B 6/21/69 M.P.G.
R&B 7/24/71 What's Going On
R&B 9/29/73 Let's Get It On
R&B 8/31/74 Marvin Gaye Live!
R&B 5/15/76 I Want You
R&B 4/30/77 Marvin Gaye Live At The London Palladium
R&B 12/4/82 Midnight Love

GEILS, J., Band

Pop 2/6/82 Freeze-Frame

GENTRY, Bobbie

C&W 10/7/67 Ode To Billie Joe
Pop 10/14/67 ↓
C&W 10/26/68 Bobbie Gentry & Glen Campbell

GETO BOYS, The

R&B 3/27/93 Till Death Do Us Part
R&B 4/20/96 The Resurrection

GETZ, Stan/Charlie Byrd

Pop 3/9/63 Jazz Samba

GHOSTFACE KILLAH

R&B 11/16/96 Ironman

GIBSON, Debbie

Pop 3/11/89 Electric Youth

GILL, Johnny

R&B 6/30/90 Johnny Gill

GILL, Vince

C&W 8/29/98 The Key

GILLEY, Mickey

C&W 11/9/74 Room Full Of Roses
C&W 2/1/75 City Lights

GINUWINE

R&B 4/26/03 The Senior

GLASER, Tompall — see JENNINGS, Waylon

GLEASON, Jackie

Pop 4/4/53 Music For Lovers Only
Pop 3/6/54 Tawny
Pop 10/30/54 Music, Martinis, and Memories
Pop 7/23/55 Lonesome Echo

GODFREY, Arthur

Pop 4/18/53 Arthur Godfrey's TV Calendar Show
Pop 12/26/53 Christmas With Arthur Godfrey And All The Little Godfreys

GODSMACK

Pop 4/26/03 Faceless

GOD'S PROPERTY

R&B 6/14/97 God's Property

GO-GO'S

Pop 3/6/82 Beauty And The Beat

GOLDSBORO, Bobby

C&W 5/25/68 Honey

GOODMAN, Benny

Pop 5/25/46 Benny Goodman Sextet Session
Pop 12/20/52 1937/38 Jazz Concert No. 2

GREEN, Al

R&B 3/18/72 Let's Stay Together
R&B 12/2/72 I'm Still In Love With You
R&B 6/9/73 Call Me
R&B 2/23/74 Livin' For You
R&B 3/22/75 Al Green Explores Your Mind
R&B 11/1/75 Al Green Is Love

GREENE, Jack

C&W 2/11/67 There Goes My Everything
C&W 7/29/67 All The Time

GREENWOOD, Lee

C&W 2/22/86 Streamline

GROBAN, Josh

Pop 1/24/04 Closer

GUNS N' ROSES

Pop 8/6/88 Appetite For Destruction
Pop 10/5/91 Use Your Illusion II

GUY

R&B 4/15/89 Guy
R&B 2/2/91 The Future

GZA/GENIUS

R&B 7/17/99 Beneath The Surface

H

HAGGARD, Merle

C&W 12/10/66 Swinging Doors and The Bottle Let Me Down
C&W 12/16/67 Branded Man
C&W 3/9/68 Sing Me Back Home
C&W 7/19/69 Same Train, A Different Time
C&W 3/21/70 Okie From Muskogee
C&W 10/10/70 The Fightin' Side Of Me
C&W 5/22/71 Hag
C&W 11/25/72 The Best Of The Best Of Merle Haggard
C&W 1/27/73 It's Not Love (But It's Not Bad)
C&W 9/22/73 I Love Dixie Blues...so I recorded "Live" in New Orleans
C&W 11/30/74 Merle Haggard Presents His 30th Album
C&W 6/14/75 Keep Movin' On
C&W 5/1/76 It's All In The Movies
C&W 4/9/83 Pancho & Lefty
MERLE HAGGARD/WILLIE NELSON
C&W 9/22/84 It's All In The Game

HALL, Tom T.

C&W 6/9/73 The Rhymer And Other Five And Dimers

HAMLISCH, Marvin

Pop 5/4/74 The Sting

HARRIS, Emmylou

C&W 4/10/76 Elite Hotel
C&W 2/26/77 Luxury Liner
C&W 5/2/87 Trio
DOLLY PARTON, LINDA RONSTADT, EMMYLOU HARRIS

HARRISON, George

Pop	1/2/71	All Things Must Pass
Pop	6/23/73	Living In The Material World

HART, Freddie

C&W	10/30/71	Easy Loving
C&W	1/13/73	Got The All Overs For You
C&W	5/19/73	Super Kind Of Woman

HAYES, Isaac

R&B	8/23/69	Hot Buttered Soul
R&B	5/16/70	The Isaac Hayes Movement
R&B	12/26/70	To Be Continued
R&B	9/25/71	Shaft
Pop	11/6/71	↓
R&B	1/15/72	Black Moses
R&B	6/23/73	Live At The Sahara Tahoe
R&B	8/9/75	Chocolate Chip

HAYMES, Dick

Pop	2/23/46	State Fair

HEART

Pop	12/21/85	Heart

HEAVY D & THE BOYZ

R&B	8/26/89	Big Tyme
R&B	6/11/94	Nuttin' But Love

HENDRIX, Jimi

Pop	11/16/68	Electric Ladyland

HI-FIVE

R&B	4/20/91	Hi-Five

HILL, Faith

Pop	11/27/99	Breathe
C&W	11/27/99	↓
Pop	11/2/02	Cry
C&W	11/2/02	↓

HILL, Lauryn

Pop	9/12/98	The Miseducation Of Lauryn Hill
R&B	9/12/98	↓

HOOTIE & THE BLOWFISH

Pop	5/27/95	Cracked Rear View
Pop	5/11/96	Fairweather Johnson

HOT BOY$

Pop	8/14/99	Guerilla Warfare

HOUSTON, David

C&W	10/8/66	Almost Persuaded

HOUSTON, Whitney

R&B	6/22/85	Whitney Houston
Pop	3/8/86	↓
Pop	6/27/87	Whitney
R&B	12/22/90	I'm Your Baby Tonight
Pop	12/12/92	The Bodyguard
R&B	12/12/92	↓
R&B	1/4/97	The Preacher's Wife

H-TOWN

R&B	5/29/93	Fever For Da Flavor

I

IAN, Janis

Pop	9/20/75	Between The Lines

ICE CUBE

R&B	12/14/91	Death Certificate

Pop	12/5/92	The Predator
R&B	12/5/92	↓
R&B	12/25/93	Lethal Injection
R&B	4/8/00	War & Peace Vol. 2 (The Peace Disc)

IMPRESSIONS, The

R&B	3/27/65	People Get Ready

INDIA.ARIE

R&B	10/12/02	Voyage To India

INK SPOTS

Pop	9/28/46	Ink Spots

INSTANT FUNK

R&B	3/31/79	Instant Funk

ISLEY BROTHERS, The

R&B	11/16/74	Live It Up
R&B	7/19/75	The Heat Is On
Pop	9/13/75	↓
R&B	6/26/76	Harvest For The World
R&B	5/14/77	Go For Your Guns
R&B	5/13/78	Showdown
R&B	5/3/80	Go All The Way
R&B	7/23/83	Between The Sheets
R&B	8/25/01	Eternal
Pop	5/24/03	Body Kiss
R&B	5/24/03	↓

J

JACKSON, Alan

C&W	8/14/93	A Lot About Livin' (And A Little 'Bout Love)
C&W	7/23/94	Who I Am
C&W	11/11/95	The Greatest Hits Collection
C&W	11/16/96	Everything I Love
C&W	9/19/98	High Mileage
C&W	11/25/00	When Somebody Loves You
Pop	2/2/02	Drive
C&W	2/2/02	↓
Pop	8/30/03	Greatest Hits Volume II and Some Other Stuff
C&W	8/30/03	↓

JACKSON, Freddie

R&B	6/29/85	Rock Me Tonight
R&B	12/6/86	Just Like The First Time
R&B	10/15/88	Don't Let Love Slip Away
R&B	2/23/91	Do Me Again

JACKSON, Janet

R&B	4/19/86	Control
Pop	7/5/86	↓
Pop	10/28/89	Janet Jackson's Rhythm Nation 1814
R&B	11/18/89	↓
Pop	6/5/93	janet.
R&B	6/5/93	↓
Pop	10/25/97	The Velvet Rope
Pop	5/12/01	All For You
R&B	5/12/01	↓

JACKSON, Jermaine

R&B	6/7/80	Let's Get Serious
R&B	7/7/84	Jermaine Jackson

JACKSON, Michael

R&B	10/6/79	Off The Wall
R&B	1/29/83	Thriller
Pop	2/26/83	↓
Pop	9/26/87	Bad
Pop	10/3/87	↓
Pop	12/14/91	Dangerous
R&B	1/4/92	↓
Pop	7/8/95	HIStory: Past, Present And Future - Book I
R&B	7/8/95	↓
Pop	11/17/01	Invincible
R&B	11/17/01	↓

JACKSON 5, The

R&B	2/14/70	Diana Ross Presents The Jackson 5
R&B	6/20/70	ABC
R&B	10/10/70	Third Album
R&B	5/8/71	Maybe Tomorrow
R&B	11/8/80	Triumph

JAGGED EDGE

R&B	2/5/00	J.E. Heartbreak
R&B	11/1/03	Hard

JAMES, Harry

Pop	1/11/47	All-Time Favorites by Harry James
Pop	5/13/50	Young Man With A Horn
		DORIS DAY and HARRY JAMES

JAMES, Rick

R&B	6/6/81	Street Songs
R&B	9/17/83	Cold Blooded

JAMES, Sonny

C&W	12/24/66	The Best Of Sonny James
C&W	7/15/67	Need You

JARREAU, Al

R&B	10/24/81	Breakin' Away

JA RULE

R&B	6/19/99	Venni Vetti Vecci
Pop	10/28/00	Rule 3:36
R&B	10/28/00	↓
Pop	10/20/01	Pain Is Love
R&B	10/20/01	↓
R&B	11/22/03	Blood In My Eye

JAY-Z

Pop	10/17/98	Vol. 2...Hard Knock Life
R&B	10/17/98	↓
Pop	1/15/00	Vol. 3...Life And Times Of S. Carter
R&B	1/15/00	↓
Pop	11/18/00	The Dynasty Roc La Familia (2000 —)
R&B	11/18/00	↓
Pop	9/29/01	The Blueprint
R&B	9/29/01	↓
R&B	4/6/02	The Best Of Both Worlds
		R. KELLY & JAY-Z
Pop	11/30/02	The Blueprint 2: The Gift And The Curse
R&B	11/30/02	↓
Pop	11/29/03	The Black Album
R&B	11/29/03	↓

JEFFERSON STARSHIP

Pop	9/6/75	Red Octopus

JENNINGS, Waylon

C&W	9/6/75	Dreaming My Dreams
C&W	2/28/76	The Outlaws
		WAYLON JENNINGS/WILLIE NELSON/JESSI COLTER/ TOMPALL GLASER
C&W	8/14/76	Are You Ready For The Country
C&W	1/15/77	Waylon Live
C&W	6/4/77	Ol' Waylon
C&W	2/25/78	Waylon & Willie
C&W	11/11/78	I've Always Been Crazy
C&W	6/2/79	Greatest Hits
C&W	7/12/80	Music Man
C&W	9/28/85	Highwayman
		WILLIE NELSON/ JOHNNY CASH/ WAYLON JENNINGS/ KRIS KRISTOFFERSON
C&W	6/14/86	Will The Wolf Survive

JETHRO TULL

Pop	6/3/72	Thick As A Brick
Pop	8/18/73	A Passion Play

JEWELL, Buddy

C&W	7/19/03	Buddy Jewell

JODECI

R&B	11/16/91	Forever My Lady
R&B	1/22/94	Diary Of A Mad Band
R&B	8/5/95	The Show - The After-Party - The Hotel

JOE

R&B	5/6/00	My Name Is Joe

JOEL, Billy

Pop	11/18/78	52nd Street
Pop	6/14/80	Glass Houses
Pop	12/16/89	Storm Front
Pop	8/28/93	River Of Dreams

JOHN, Elton

Pop	7/15/72	Honky Chateau
Pop	3/3/73	Don't Shoot Me I'm Only The Piano Player
Pop	11/10/73	Goodbye Yellow Brick Road
Pop	7/13/74	Caribou
Pop	11/30/74	Elton John - Greatest Hits
Pop	6/7/75	Captain Fantastic And The Brown Dirt Cowboy
Pop	11/8/75	Rock Of The Westies

JOLSON, Al

Pop	2/1/47	Al Jolson in songs he made famous
Pop	8/16/47	Al Jolson Souvenir Album
Pop	7/24/48	Al Jolson - Volume Three

JONES, George

C&W	8/6/66	I'm A People
C&W	10/30/76	Golden Ring
		GEORGE JONES & TAMMY WYNETTE

JONES, Norah

Pop	1/25/03	Come Away With Me
Pop	2/28/04	Feels Like Home

JONES, Quincy

R&B	7/6/74	Body Heat
R&B	1/27/90	Back On The Block

JOPLIN, Janis

Pop	2/27/71	Pearl

JOURNEY

Pop	9/12/81	Escape

JUDDS, The

C&W	2/2/85	Why Not Me
C&W	3/1/86	Rockin' With The Rhythm
C&W	3/21/87	Heartland
C&W	10/29/88	Greatest Hits

JUVENILE

R&B	1/1/00	Tha G-Code

K

KAEMPFERT, Bert, And His Orchestra

Pop	1/16/61	Wonderland By Night

KANE & ABEL

R&B	7/25/98	Am I My Brothers Keeper

KAYE, Danny

Pop	2/14/53	Hans Christian Andersen

KC AND THE SUNSHINE BAND

R&B	11/15/75	KC And The Sunshine Band

KEITH, Toby

C&W	9/15/01	Pull My Chain
Pop	8/10/02	Unleashed
C&W	8/10/02	↓
Pop	11/22/03	Shock'n Y'all
C&W	11/22/03	↓

KELLY, R.

R&B	2/5/94	12 Play
Pop	12/2/95	R. Kelly
R&B	12/2/95	↓
R&B	11/28/98	R.
Pop	11/25/00	TP-2.com
R&B	11/25/00	↓
R&B	4/6/02	The Best Of Both Worlds
		R. KELLY & JAY-Z
Pop	3/8/03	Chocolate Factory
R&B	3/8/03	↓

KENDRICKS, Eddie

R&B	4/27/74	Boogie Down!

KENNY G

Pop	12/10/94	Miracles - The Holiday Album
R&B	12/24/94	↓

KENTON, Stan

Pop	5/29/48	A Presentation Of Progressive Jazz

KEYS, Alicia

Pop	7/14/01	Songs In A Minor
R&B	7/14/01	↓
Pop	12/20/03	The Diary Of Alicia Keys
R&B	12/20/03	↓

KING, B.B.

R&B	4/10/71	Live In Cook County Jail

KING, Carole

Pop	6/19/71	Tapestry
Pop	1/1/72	Music
Pop	11/9/74	Wrap Around Joy

KING, Evelyn

R&B	10/23/82	Get Loose

KINGSTON TRIO, The

Pop	11/24/58	The Kingston Trio
Pop	7/27/59	The Kingston Trio At Large
Pop	12/14/59	Here We Go Again!
Pop	5/9/60	Sold Out
Pop	8/29/60	String Along

KNACK, The

Pop	8/11/79	Get The Knack

KNIGHT, Gladys, & The Pips

R&B	4/14/73	Neither One Of Us
R&B	12/15/73	Imagination
R&B	7/13/74	Claudine
R&B	12/28/74	I Feel A Song
R&B	2/27/88	All Our Love
R&B	10/19/91	Good Woman
		GLADYS KNIGHT

KOOL & THE GANG

R&B	10/27/79	Ladies' Night
R&B	11/21/81	Something Special

KOOL G RAP

R&B	10/14/95	4,5,6

KORN

Pop	9/5/98	Follow The Leader
Pop	12/4/99	Issues

KRIS KROSS

Pop	5/23/92	Totally Krossed Out
R&B	5/23/92	↓

KRISTOFFERSON, Kris

C&W	11/3/73	Jesus Was A Capricorn
C&W	11/10/73	Full Moon
		KRIS KRISTOFFERSON & RITA COOLIDGE
C&W	9/28/85	Highwayman
		WILLIE NELSON/ JOHNNY CASH/ WAYLON JENNINGS/ KRIS KRISTOFFERSON

L

LaBELLE, Patti

R&B	6/14/86	Winner In You
Pop	7/19/86	↓

LANZA, Mario

Pop	2/24/51	The Toast Of New Orleans
Pop	6/2/51	The Great Caruso
Pop	12/22/51	Mario Lanza sings Christmas songs
Pop	11/15/52	Because You're Mine
Pop	8/21/54	The Student Prince and other great musical comedies

LED ZEPPELIN

Pop	12/27/69	Led Zeppelin II
Pop	10/31/70	Led Zeppelin III
Pop	5/12/73	Houses Of The Holy
Pop	3/22/75	Physical Graffiti
Pop	5/1/76	Presence
Pop	9/15/79	In Through The Out Door
Pop	6/14/03	How The West Was Won

LENNON, John
Pop 10/30/71 Imagine
Pop 11/16/74 Walls And Bridges
Pop 12/27/80 Double Fantasy
JOHN LENNON YOKO ONO

LEVERT, Gerald
R&B 4/18/92 Private Line
R&B 11/15/03 Stroke Of Genius

LEWIS, Huey, and The News
Pop 6/30/84 Sports
Pop 10/18/86 Fore!

LEWIS, Ramsey
R&B 9/11/65 The In Crowd
R&B 5/24/75 Sun Goddess

LIBERACE
Pop 10/25/52 Liberace at the piano

LIGHT, Enoch, & The Light Brigade
Pop 4/25/60 Persuasive Percussion
TERRY SNYDER & THE ALL-STARS
Pop 11/20/61 Stereo 35/MM

LIGHTFOOT, Gordon
Pop 6/22/74 Sundown

LIL' KIM
R&B 7/15/00 The Notorious KIM

LIL WAYNE
R&B 11/20/99 Tha Block Is Hot
R&B 8/10/02 500 Degreez

LIMP BIZKIT
Pop 7/10/99 Significant Other
Pop 11/4/00 Chocolate Starfish And The Hot Dog Flavored Water

LINKIN PARK
Pop 4/12/03 Meteora

LIVE
Pop 5/6/95 Throwing Copper
Pop 3/8/97 Secret Samadhi

LL COOL J
R&B 7/11/87 Bigger And Deffer
R&B 7/22/89 Walking With A Panther
R&B 4/17/93 14 Shots To The Dome
Pop 9/30/00 G.O.A.T. Featuring James T. Smith The Greatest Of All Time
R&B 9/30/00 ↓
R&B 11/2/02 10

LONESTAR
C&W 7/14/01 I'm Already There
C&W 6/21/03 From There To Here: Greatest Hits

LOPEZ, Jennifer
Pop 2/10/01 J.Lo
R&B 2/10/01 ↓
Pop 2/23/02 J To Tha L-O! The Remixes
R&B 2/23/02 ↓

LOS LOBOS
Pop 9/12/87 La Bamba

LOST BOYZ
R&B 6/22/96 Legal Drug Money

LOX, The
R&B 1/31/98 Money, Power & Respect

L.T.D.
R&B 10/8/77 Something To Love

LUDACRIS
R&B 12/15/01 Word Of Mouf
Pop 10/25/03 Chicken*N*Beer
R&B 10/25/03 ↓

LUNIZ
R&B 7/22/95 Operation Stackola

LYNN, Loretta
C&W 11/12/66 You Ain't Woman Enough
C&W 5/20/67 Don't Come Home A'Drinkin' (With Lovin' On Your Mind)
C&W 6/15/68 Fist City
C&W 6/2/73 Entertainer Of The Year-Loretta
C&W 9/15/73 Louisiana Woman-Mississippi Man
CONWAY TWITTY-LORETTA LYNN
C&W 10/27/73 Love Is The · Fonundation
C&W 9/21/74 Country Partners
C&W 8/16/75 Feelins'
C&W 8/7/76 United Talent
LORETTA LYNN/CONWAY TWITTY (above 3)
C&W 12/11/76 Somebody Somewhere

M

MADONNA
Pop 2/9/85 Like A Virgin
Pop 8/16/86 True Blue
Pop 4/22/89 Like A Prayer
Pop 10/7/00 Music
Pop 5/10/03 American Life

MAMAS & THE PAPAS, The
Pop 5/21/66 If You Can Believe Your Eyes And Ears

MANCINI, Henry
Pop 2/23/59 The Music From Peter Gunn
Pop 2/10/62 Breakfast At Tiffany's

MANILOW, Barry
Pop 7/16/77 Barry Manilow/Live

MANSON, Marilyn
Pop 10/3/98 Mechanical Animals
Pop 5/31/03 The Golden Age Of Grotesque

MANTOVANI
Pop 6/6/53 The Music of Victor Herbert
Pop 7/13/59 Film Encores

MARTIN, Ricky
Pop 5/29/99 Ricky Martin

MARX, Richard
Pop 9/2/89 Repeat Offender

MA$E
Pop 11/15/97 Harlem World
R&B 11/15/97 ↓

MASTER P
Pop 9/20/97 Ghetto D
R&B 9/20/97 ↓
Pop 6/20/98 MP Da Last Don
R&B 6/20/98 ↓
R&B 11/13/99 Only God Can Judge Me

MATHIS, Johnny
Pop 6/9/58 Johnny's Greatest Hits
Pop 11/9/59 Heavenly

MATTHEWS, Dave, Band
Pop 5/16/98 Before These Crowded Streets
Pop 3/17/01 Everyday
Pop 8/3/02 Busted Stuff

MAURIAT, Paul
Pop 3/2/68 Blooming Hits

MAXWELL
Pop 9/8/01 Now
R&B 9/8/01 ↓

MAYER, John
Pop 9/27/03 Heavier Things

MAYFIELD, Curtis
R&B 2/6/71 Curtis
R&B 10/14/72 Superfly
Pop 10/21/72 ↓
R&B 7/21/73 Back To The World

MAZE Featuring Frankie Beverly
R&B 4/27/85 Can't Stop The Love
R&B 11/11/89 Silky Soul

MC EIHT FEATURING CMW
R&B 8/6/94 We Come Strapped

M.C. HAMMER
R&B 4/8/89 Let's Get It Started
R&B 4/28/90 Please Hammer Don't Hurt 'Em
Pop 6/9/90 ↓

MC REN
R&B 12/4/93 Shock Of The Hour

McBRIDE, Martina
C&W 10/6/01 Greatest Hits
C&W 10/18/03 Martina

McCALL, C.W.
C&W 12/27/75 Black Bear Road

McCARTNEY, Paul/Wings
Pop 5/23/70 McCartney
Pop 6/2/73 Red Rose Speedway
Pop 4/13/74 Band On The Run
PAUL McCARTNEY & WINGS (above 2)
Pop 7/19/75 Venus And Mars
Pop 4/24/76 Wings At The Speed Of Sound
Pop 1/22/77 Wings Over America
WINGS (above 3)
Pop 5/29/82 Tug Of War
PAUL McCARTNEY

McCOY, Charlie
C&W 7/7/73 Good Time Charlie

McCOY, Van, & The Soul City Symphony
R&B 7/12/75 Disco Baby

McENTIRE, Reba
C&W 5/24/86 Whoever's In New England
C&W 1/24/87 What Am I Gonna Do About You
C&W 6/11/88 Reba
C&W 6/24/89 Sweet Sixteen
C&W 5/22/93 It's Your Call
C&W 1/22/94 Greatest Hits Volume Two
C&W 10/21/95 Starting Over
C&W 11/30/96 What If It's You
C&W 11/10/01 Greatest Hits Volume III - I'm A Survivor

McGRAW, Tim
C&W 4/9/94 Not A Moment Too Soon
Pop 5/21/94 ↓
C&W 10/7/95 All I Want
C&W 6/21/97 Everywhere
Pop 5/22/99 A Place In The Sun
C&W 5/22/99 ↓
C&W 12/9/00 Greatest Hits
C&W 5/12/01 Set This Circus Down

McKNIGHT, Brian
R&B 2/14/98 Anytime

McLEAN, Don
Pop 1/22/72 American Pie

MEADER, Vaughn
Pop 12/15/62 The First Family

MEAT LOAF
Pop 10/30/93 Bat Out Of Hell II: Back Into Hell

MELLENCAMP, John Cougar
Pop 9/11/82 American Fool

MELVIN, Harold, And The Blue Notes
R&B 5/10/75 To Be True
R&B 1/24/76 Wake Up Everybody

MEMPHIS BLEEK
R&B 8/21/99 Coming Of Age
R&B 12/23/00 The Understanding

MEN AT WORK
Pop 11/13/82 Business As Usual

MESSINA, Jo Dee
C&W 8/19/00 Burn
C&W 6/7/03 Greatest Hits

METALLICA
Pop 8/31/91 Metallica
Pop 6/22/96 Load
Pop 12/6/97 Reload
Pop 6/21/03 St. Anger

METHOD MAN
R&B 12/3/94 Tical
R&B 12/5/98 Tical 2000: Judgement Day
R&B 10/16/99 Blackout!
METHOD MAN/REDMAN

MFSB
R&B 3/16/74 Love Is The Message

MICHAEL, George/ Wham!
Pop 3/2/85 Make It Big
WHAM!

Pop 1/16/88 Faith
GEORGE MICHAEL
R&B 5/21/88 ↓

MILLER, Glenn, and his Orchestra
Pop 5/12/45 Glenn Miller
Pop 11/8/47 Glenn Miller Masterpieces
Pop 3/13/54 The Glenn Miller Story
Pop 3/20/54 Glenn Miller Plays Selections From The Film "The Glenn Miller Story"

MILLER, Mitch, & The Gang
Pop 10/6/58 Sing Along With Mitch
Pop 12/29/58 Christmas Sing-Along With Mitch
Pop 1/6/62 Holiday Sing Along With Mitch

MILLER, Roger
C&W 9/25/65 The 3rd Time Around

MILLI VANILLI
Pop 9/23/89 Girl You Know It's True

MILLS, Stephanie
R&B 9/5/87 If I Were Your Woman

MILSAP, Ronnie
C&W 12/20/80 Greatest Hits
C&W 10/17/81 There's No Gettin' Over Me
C&W 9/7/85 Greatest Hits, Vol. 2
C&W 6/21/86 Lost In The Fifties Tonight

MIRACLES, The
R&B 1/15/66 Going To A Go-Go
R&B 12/7/68 Special Occasion

MR. MISTER
Pop 3/1/86 Welcome To The Real World

MR. SERV-ON
R&B 3/6/99 Da Next Level

MOBB DEEP
R&B 12/7/96 Hell On Earth
R&B 12/29/01 Infamy

MONICA
Pop 7/5/03 After The Storm

MONKEES, The
Pop 11/12/66 The Monkees
Pop 2/11/67 More Of The Monkees
Pop 6/24/67 Headquarters
Pop 12/2/67 Pisces, Aquarius, Capricorn & Jones Ltd.

MONROE, Vaughn
Pop 12/1/45 On The Moon-Beam
Pop 4/3/48 Down Memory Lane
Pop 1/22/49 Vaughn Monroe Sings

MONTGOMERY, John Michael
C&W 2/12/94 Kickin' It Up
Pop 2/19/94 ↓
C&W 4/15/95 John Michael Montgomery

MOODY BLUES, The
Pop 12/9/72 Seventh Sojourn

Pop 7/25/81 Long Distance Voyager

MORISSETTE, Alanis
Pop 10/7/95 Jagged Little Pill
Pop 11/21/98 Supposed Former Infatuation Junkie
Pop 3/16/02 Under Rug Swept

MORMON TABERNACLE CHOIR, The
Pop 1/11/60 The Lord's Prayer

MORRIS, Gary
C&W 12/21/85 Anything Goes...

MÖTLEY CRÜE
Pop 10/14/89 Dr. Feelgood

MUSIQ
Pop 5/25/02 JUSLISEN (Just Listen)
R&B 5/25/02 ↓

MYSTIKAL
R&B 11/29/97 Unpredictable
R&B 1/2/99 Ghetto Fabulous
Pop 10/14/00 Let's Get Ready
R&B 10/14/00 ↓

N

NAS
Pop 7/20/96 It Was Written
R&B 7/20/96 ↓
Pop 4/24/99 I Am...
R&B 4/24/99 ↓
R&B 1/5/02 Stillmatic
R&B 1/4/03 God's Son

NAUGHTY BY NATURE
R&B 3/13/93 19 Naughty III
R&B 6/17/95 Poverty's Paradise

NELLY
R&B 8/5/00 Country Grammar
Pop 8/26/00 ↓
Pop 7/13/02 Nellyville
R&B 7/13/02 ↓

NELSON, Ricky
Pop 1/20/58 Ricky

NELSON, Willie
C&W 10/4/75 Red Headed Stranger
C&W 2/28/76 The Outlaws
WAYLON JENNINGS/WILLIE NELSON/JESSI COLTER/ TOMPALL GLASER
C&W 4/24/76 The Sound In Your Mind
C&W 11/20/76 The Troublemaker
C&W 2/25/78 Waylon & Willie
C&W 6/10/78 Stardust
C&W 1/6/79 Willie and Family Live
C&W 10/4/80 Honeysuckle Rose
WILLIE NELSON & FAMILY
C&W 5/2/81 Somewhere Over The Rainbow
C&W 12/5/81 Willie Nelson's Greatest Hits (& Some That Will Be)
C&W 5/22/82 Always On My Mind
C&W 4/9/83 Pancho & Lefty
MERLE HAGGARD/WILLIE NELSON
C&W 9/29/84 City Of New Orleans

NELSON, Willie — Cont'd

C&W 9/28/85 Highwayman
WILLIE NELSON/
JOHNNY CASH/
WAYLON JENNINGS/
KRIS KRISTOFFERSON
C&W 5/31/86 The Promiseland

NEW BIRTH, The

R&B 6/2/73 Birth Day

NEW EDITION

R&B 1/5/85 New Edition
Pop 9/28/96 Home Again
R&B 9/28/96 ↓

NEWHART, Bob

Pop 7/25/60 The Button-Down
Mind Of Bob
Newhart
Pop 1/9/61 The Button-Down
Mind Strikes Back!

NEW KIDS ON THE BLOCK

Pop 9/9/89 Hangin' Tough
Pop 6/30/90 Step By Step

NEWTON-JOHN, Olivia

C&W 3/2/74 Let Me Be There
C&W 7/13/74 If You Love Me, Let
Me Know
Pop 10/12/74 ↓
Pop 3/15/75 Have You Never
Been Mellow
C&W 3/22/75 ↓

NICKS, Stevie

Pop 9/5/81 Bella Donna

NINE INCH NAILS

Pop 10/9/99 The Fragile

NIRVANA

Pop 1/11/92 Nevermind
Pop 10/9/93 In Utero
Pop 11/19/94 MTV Unplugged In
New York
Pop 10/19/96 From The Muddy
Banks Of The
Wishkah

NO DOUBT

Pop 12/21/96 Tragic Kingdom

NOREAGA

R&B 8/1/98 N.O.R.E.

NOTORIOUS B.I.G., The

Pop 4/12/97 Life After Death
R&B 4/12/97 ↓
Pop 12/25/99 Born Again
R&B 12/25/99 ↓

*NSYNC

Pop 4/8/00 No Strings Attached
Pop 8/11/01 Celebrity

N.W.A.

Pop 6/22/91 EFIL4ZAGGIN

O

OAK RIDGE BOYS

C&W 7/18/81 Fancy Free
C&W 3/27/82 Bobbie Sue
C&W 4/28/84 Deliver

OCEAN, Billy

R&B 8/9/86 Love Zone

O'CONNOR, Sinéad

Pop 4/28/90 I Do Not Want What I
Haven't Got

OHIO PLAYERS

R&B 7/20/74 Skin Tight
R&B 1/4/75 Fire
Pop 2/8/75 ↓
R&B 9/27/75 Honey
R&B 7/24/76 Contradiction

O'JAYS, The

R&B 2/16/74 Ship Ahoy
R&B 6/7/75 Survival
R&B 12/27/75 Family Reunion
R&B 6/3/78 So Full Of Love

112

R&B 4/7/01 Part III

ONE WAY

R&B 7/14/84 Lady

ONO, Yoko — see LENNON, John

OSLIN, K.T.

C&W 2/27/88 80's Ladies

OSMOND, Marie

C&W 11/17/73 Paper Roses

OUTKAST

R&B 9/14/96 ATLiens
Pop 10/11/03 Speakerboxxx/The
Love Below
R&B 10/11/03 ↓

OWENS, Buck, And His Buckaroos

C&W 1/25/64 Buck Owens Sings
Tommy Collins
C&W 11/21/64 Together Again/My
Heart Skips A Beat
C&W 1/9/65 I Don't Care
C&W 4/10/65 I've Got A Tiger By
The Tail
C&W 10/9/65 Before You Go/No
One But You
C&W 4/9/66 Roll out the red
carpet for Buck
Owens and his
Buckaroos
C&W 8/20/66 Dust On Mother's Bible
C&W 9/10/66 Carnegie Hall Concert
C&W 3/18/67 Open Up Your Heart
C&W 7/22/67 Buck Owens And His
Buckaroos In Japan!
C&W 10/28/67 Your Tender Loving
Care
C&W 3/16/68 It Takes People Like
You To Make
People Like Me

P

PAISLEY, Brad

C&W 8/9/03 Mud On The Tires

PANTERA

Pop 4/9/94 Far Beyond Driven

PARKER, Ray Jr./Raydio

R&B 5/23/81 A Woman Needs
Love
R&B 5/29/82 The Other Woman

PARTON, Dolly

C&W 5/14/77 New Harvest...First
Gathering
C&W 12/24/77 Here You Come
Again
C&W 9/9/78 Heartbreaker
C&W 2/14/81 9 To 5 And Odd Jobs
C&W 5/2/87 Trio
DOLLY PARTON, LINDA
RONSTADT, EMMYLOU
HARRIS
C&W 5/18/91 Eagle When She
Flies

PAUL, Billy

R&B 1/6/73 360 Degrees Of Billy
Paul

PEACHES & HERB

R&B 3/3/79 2 Hot!

PEARL JAM

Pop 11/6/93 Vs.
Pop 12/24/94 Vitalogy
Pop 9/14/96 No Code

PENDERGRASS, Teddy

R&B 8/12/78 Life Is A Song Worth
Singing
R&B 7/21/79 Teddy

PETER, PAUL & MARY

Pop 10/20/62 Peter, Paul and Mary
Pop 11/2/63 In The Wind

PINK FLOYD

Pop 4/28/73 The Dark Side Of The
Moon
Pop 10/4/75 Wish You Were Here
Pop 1/19/80 The Wall
Pop 4/23/94 The Division Bell
Pop 6/24/95 Pulse

POLICE, The

Pop 7/23/83 Synchronicity

PRESLEY, Elvis

Pop 5/5/56 Elvis Presley
Pop 12/8/56 Elvis
Pop 7/29/57 Loving You
Pop 12/16/57 Elvis' Christmas Album
Pop 12/5/60 G.I. Blues
Pop 8/21/61 Something for
Everybody
Pop 12/11/61 Blue Hawaii
Pop 1/2/65 Roustabout
C&W 4/14/73 Aloha from Hawaii via
Satellite
Pop 5/5/73 ↓
C&W 3/30/74 Elvis-A Legendary
Performer, Volume 1
C&W 3/8/75 Promised Land
C&W 7/10/76 From Elvis Presley
Boulevard, Memphis,
Tennessee
C&W 9/3/77 Moody Blue
C&W 11/12/77 Elvis In Concert
Pop 10/12/02 Elv1s: 30 #1 Hits
C&W 10/12/02 ↓

PRICE, Ray

C&W 1/18/64 Night Life
C&W 11/5/66 Another Bridge To
Burn
C&W 4/29/67 Touch My Heart
C&W 11/28/70 For The Good Times
C&W 7/3/71 I Won't Mention It
Again

PRIDE, Charley

C&W	5/18/68	The Country Way
C&W	12/20/69	The Best Of Charley Pride
C&W	4/25/70	Just Plain Charley
C&W	8/8/70	Charley Pride's 10th Album
C&W	6/26/71	Did You Think To Pray
C&W	8/14/71	I'm Just Me
C&W	1/1/72	Charley Pride Sings Heart Songs
C&W	4/22/72	The Best Of Charley Pride, Volume 2
C&W	9/16/72	A Sunshiny Day with Charley Pride
C&W	2/17/73	Songs of Love by Charley Pride
C&W	2/16/74	Amazing Love
C&W	5/3/80	There's A Little Bit Of Hank In Me

PRINCE

R&B	7/28/84	Purple Rain
Pop	8/4/84	↓
Pop	6/1/85	Around The World In A Day
Pop	7/22/89	Batman
R&B	12/7/91	Diamonds And Pearls

PRODIGY

Pop	7/19/97	The Fat Of The Land

PRUETT, Jeanne

C&W	7/21/73	Satin Sheets

PRYOR, Richard

R&B	9/7/74	That Nigger's Crazy
R&B	10/11/75	Is It Something I Said?

PUBLIC ENEMY

R&B	9/24/88	It Takes A Nation Of Millions To Hold Us Back
R&B	11/23/91	Apocalypse 91...The Enemy Strikes Black

PUFF DADDY

Pop	8/9/97	No Way Out
		PUFF DADDY & THE FAMILY
R&B	8/9/97	↓
R&B	9/11/99	Forever

Q

QUEEN

Pop	9/20/80	The Game

QUIET RIOT

Pop	11/26/83	Metal Health

R

RABBITT, Eddie

C&W	9/13/80	Horizon
C&W	9/26/81	Step By Step

RADIOHEAD

Pop	10/21/00	Kid A

RAFFERTY, Gerry

Pop	7/8/78	City to City

RAGE AGAINST THE MACHINE

Pop	5/4/96	Evil Empire
Pop	11/20/99	The Battle Of Los Angeles

RAITT, Bonnie

Pop	4/7/90	Nick Of Time
Pop	4/16/94	Longing In Their Hearts

RAKIM

R&B	11/22/97	The 18th Letter

RANKS, Shabba

R&B	11/9/91	As Raw As Ever

RASCAL FLATTS

C&W	11/16/02	Melt

RASCALS, The

Pop	9/28/68	Time Peace/The Rascals' Greatest Hits

RAWLS, Lou

R&B	5/21/66	Lou Rawls Live!
R&B	10/1/66	Lou Rawls Soulin'
R&B	8/21/76	All Things In Time

REDDING, Otis

R&B	10/30/65	Otis Blue/Otis Redding Sings Soul
R&B	2/24/68	History Of Otis Redding
R&B	4/20/68	The Dock Of The Bay

REDMAN

R&B	12/10/94	Dare Iz A Darkside
R&B	12/28/96	Muddy Waters
R&B	12/26/98	Doc's Da Name 2000
R&B	10/16/99	Blackout!
		METHOD MAN/REDMAN
R&B	6/9/01	Malpractice

REEVES, Jim

C&W	7/4/64	Moonlight and Roses
C&W	9/26/64	The Best Of Jim Reeves
C&W	10/16/65	Up Through The Years
C&W	6/18/66	Distant Drums

R.E.M.

Pop	5/18/91	Out Of Time
Pop	10/15/94	Monster

REO SPEEDWAGON

Pop	2/21/81	Hi Infidelity

RESTLESS HEART

C&W	4/18/87	Wheels

RICH, Charlie

C&W	6/16/73	Behind Closed Doors
C&W	4/13/74	There Won't Be Anymore
C&W	4/27/74	Very Special Love Songs
C&W	1/11/75	The Silver Fox
C&W	8/23/75	Every Time You Touch Me (I Get High)

RICHIE, Lionel

R&B	11/27/82	Lionel Richie
R&B	11/26/83	Can't Slow Down
Pop	12/3/83	↓
Pop	9/27/86	Dancing On The Ceiling

RILEY, Jeannie C.

C&W	11/2/68	Harper Valley P.T.A.

RIMES, LeAnn

C&W	7/27/96	Blue

Pop	3/1/97	Unchained Melody/ The Early Years
C&W	3/1/97	↓
Pop	9/27/97	You Light Up My Life - Inspirational Songs
C&W	9/27/97	↓
C&W	11/13/99	LeAnn Rimes
C&W	2/17/01	I Need You

RIPERTON, Minnie

R&B	3/29/75	Perfect Angel

ROBBINS, Marty

C&W	11/13/76	El Paso City

ROBINSON, Smokey

R&B	4/18/81	Being With You
R&B	7/4/87	One Heartbeat

RODRIGUEZ, Johnny

C&W	5/26/73	Introducing Johnny Rodriguez

ROGER

R&B	11/7/81	The Many Facets Of Roger

ROGERS, Kenny

C&W	5/21/77	Kenny Rogers
C&W	4/15/78	Ten Years Of Gold
C&W	5/20/78	Every Time Two Fools Collide
		KENNY ROGERS & DOTTIE WEST
C&W	8/26/78	Love Or Something Like It
C&W	1/20/79	The Gambler
C&W	11/10/79	Kenny
C&W	5/10/80	Gideon
C&W	11/15/80	Kenny Rogers' Greatest Hits
Pop	12/13/80	↓
C&W	8/29/81	Share Your Love
C&W	10/29/83	Eyes That See In The Dark
C&W	12/28/85	The Heart Of The Matter

ROLLING STONES, The

Pop	8/21/65	Out Of Our Heads
Pop	5/22/71	Sticky Fingers
Pop	6/17/72	Exile On Main St.
Pop	10/13/73	Goats Head Soup
Pop	11/23/74	It's Only Rock 'N Roll
Pop	5/15/76	Black And Blue
Pop	7/15/78	Some Girls
Pop	7/26/80	Emotional Rescue
Pop	9/19/81	Tattoo You

RONSTADT, Linda

C&W	2/8/75	Heart Like A Wheel
Pop	2/15/75	↓
C&W	10/2/76	Hasten Down The Wind
Pop	12/3/77	Simple Dreams
C&W	12/17/77	↓
Pop	11/4/78	Living In The USA
C&W	5/2/87	Trio
		DOLLY PARTON, LINDA RONSTADT, EMMYLOU HARRIS

ROSE, David, and His Orchestra

Pop	8/31/46	a Cole Porter review

ROSE ROYCE

R&B	10/1/77	Rose Royce II/In Full Bloom

ROSS, Diana

R&B	9/26/70	Diana Ross
Pop	4/7/73	Lady Sings The Blues
R&B	8/25/73	Touch Me In The Morning
R&B	7/26/80	Diana

RUFFIN, David

R&B	7/12/69	My Whole World Ended

RUFF RYDERS

Pop	5/15/99	Ruff Ryders - Ryde Or Die Vol. I
R&B	5/15/99	↓
R&B	7/22/00	Ruff Ryders - Ryde Or Die Vol. II

RUFUS Featuring Chaka Khan

R&B	2/28/76	Rufus Featuring Chaka Khan
R&B	3/12/77	Ask Rufus
R&B	4/15/78	Street Player
R&B	12/22/79	Masterjam

RUN-D.M.C.

R&B	8/16/86	Raising Hell
R&B	5/22/93	Down With The King

S

SADE

R&B	2/1/86	Promise
Pop	2/15/86	↓

SADLER, SSgt Barry

Pop	3/12/66	Ballads of the Green Berets
C&W	3/26/66	↓

ST. LUNATICS

R&B	6/23/01	Free City

SAM & DAVE

R&B	8/20/66	Hold On, I'm Comin'

SANTANA

Pop	10/24/70	Abraxas
Pop	11/13/71	Santana III
Pop	10/30/99	Supernatural
Pop	11/9/02	Shaman

SCARFACE

R&B	9/4/93	The World Is Yours
Pop	3/29/97	The Untouchable
R&B	3/29/97	↓
R&B	3/21/98	My Homies
R&B	8/24/02	The Fix

SCHNEIDER, John

C&W	4/19/86	A Memory Like You

SEALS, Dan

C&W	3/8/86	Won't Be Blue Anymore

SEGER, Bob

Pop	5/3/80	Against The Wind

SELENA

Pop	8/5/95	Dreaming Of You

SHAGGY

R&B	2/3/01	Hotshot
Pop	2/17/01	↓

SHALAMAR

R&B	4/24/82	Friends

SHAY, Dorothy

Pop	8/2/47	Dorothy Shay (The Park Avenue Hillbillie) Sings
Pop	1/24/48	Dorothy Shay (The Park Avenue Hillbillie) Goes To Town

SHELTON, Ricky Van

C&W	3/5/88	Wild-Eyed Dream
C&W	11/5/88	Loving Proof
C&W	3/3/90	RVS III

SHERMAN, Allan

Pop	12/1/62	My Son, The Folk Singer
Pop	3/9/63	My Son, The Celebrity
Pop	8/31/63	My Son, The Nut

SILK

R&B	4/10/93	Lose Control

SILKK THE SHOCKER

R&B	3/7/98	Charge It 2 Da Game
Pop	2/6/99	Made Man
R&B	2/6/99	↓

SILVER CONVENTION

R&B	11/29/75	Save Me

SIMON, Carly

Pop	1/13/73	No Secrets

SIMON, Paul

Pop	12/6/75	Still Crazy After All These Years

SIMON & GARFUNKEL

Pop	4/6/68	The Graduate
Pop	5/25/68	Bookends
Pop	3/7/70	Bridge Over Troubled Water

SINATRA, Frank

Pop	4/6/46	The Voice of Frank Sinatra
Pop	6/25/55	in the Wee Small Hours
Pop	2/10/58	Come Fly with me
Pop	10/13/58	Frank Sinatra sings for Only The Lonely
Pop	10/24/60	Nice 'n' Easy
Pop	7/23/66	Strangers In The Night

SINGING NUN, The

Pop	12/7/63	The Singing Nun

SISTER SLEDGE

R&B	4/7/79	We Are Family

SKAGGS, Ricky

C&W	11/20/82	Highways & Heartaches
C&W	2/25/84	Don't Cheat In Our Hometown
C&W	2/23/85	Country Boy
C&W	3/29/86	Live In London

SKID ROW

Pop	6/29/91	Slave To The Grind

SKYY

R&B	2/13/82	Skyy Line

SLACK, Freddie

Pop	9/15/45	Freddie Slack's Boogie Woogie

SLICK RICK

R&B	5/13/89	The Great Adventures Of Slick Rick
R&B	6/12/99	The Art Of Storytelling

SLY & THE FAMILY STONE

R&B	12/19/70	Greatest Hits
Pop	12/18/71	There's A Riot Goin' On
R&B	1/1/72	↓
R&B	8/4/73	Fresh

SMASHING PUMPKINS, The

Pop	11/11/95	Mellon Collie And The Infinite Sadness

SMITH, Connie

C&W	7/10/65	Connie Smith
C&W	12/25/65	Cute 'n' Country
C&W	12/3/66	Born To Sing

SMITH, Jimmy

R&B	4/30/66	Got My Mojo Workin'

SMITH, O.C.

R&B	11/23/68	Hickory Holler Revisited

SMITH, Sammi

C&W	5/8/71	Help Me Make It Through The Night

SNOOP DOGG

Pop	12/11/93	Doggy Style SNOOP DOGGY DOGG
R&B	12/11/93	↓
Pop	11/30/96	Tha Doggfather SNOOP DOGGY DOGG
R&B	11/30/96	↓
Pop	8/22/98	Da Game Is To Be Sold, Not To Be Told
R&B	8/22/98	↓
R&B	5/29/99	No Limit Top Dogg
R&B	1/6/01	Tha Last Meal

SNOW, Hank

C&W	6/20/64	More Hank Snow Souvenirs

SOUL II SOUL

R&B	9/2/89	Keep On Movin'

SOUNDGARDEN

Pop	3/26/94	Superunknown

SOVINE, Red

C&W	8/28/76	Teddy Bear

SPEARS, Britney

Pop	1/30/99	...Baby One More Time
Pop	6/3/00	Oops!...I Did It Again
Pop	11/24/01	Britney
Pop	12/6/03	In The Zone

SPICE GIRLS

Pop	5/24/97	Spice

SPICE 1

R&B	10/16/93	187 He Wrote

SPINNERS

R&B	5/12/73	Spinners
R&B	6/1/74	Mighty Love
R&B	2/15/75	New And Improved

SPRINGSTEEN, Bruce

Pop	11/8/80	The River
Pop	7/7/84	Born In The U.S.A.
Pop	11/29/86	Bruce Springsteen & The E Street Band Live/1975-85
Pop	11/7/87	Tunnel of Love
Pop	3/18/95	Greatest Hits
Pop	8/17/02	The Rising

STAIND
Pop 6/9/01 Break The Cycle
Pop 6/7/03 14 Shades Of Grey

STAPLE SINGERS, The
R&B 12/6/75 Let's Do It Again

STATLER BROTHERS, The
C&W 10/19/85 Pardners in Rhyme

STEVENS, Cat
Pop 11/18/72 Catch Bull At Four

STEVENS, Ray
C&W 3/15/86 I Have Returned

STEWART, Rod
Pop 10/2/71 Every Picture Tells A Story
Pop 2/10/79 Blondes Have More Fun

STEWART, Wynn
C&W 8/26/67 It's Such A Pretty World Today

STONE TEMPLE PILOTS
Pop 6/25/94 Purple

STRAIT, George
C&W 2/18/84 Right Or Wrong
C&W 1/19/85 Does Fort Worth Ever Cross Your Mind
C&W 12/14/85 Something Special
C&W 7/12/86 #7
C&W 2/14/87 Ocean Front Property
C&W 11/7/87 Greatest Hits, Volume Two
C&W 4/23/88 If You Ain't Lovin' You Ain't Livin'
C&W 4/29/89 Beyond The Blue Neon
C&W 7/14/90 Livin' It Up
C&W 7/3/93 Pure Country
C&W 11/26/94 Lead On
C&W 5/11/96 Blue Clear Sky
C&W 5/10/97 Carrying Your Love With Me
Pop 5/17/97 ↓
C&W 5/9/98 One Step At A Time
C&W 3/25/00 Latest Greatest Straitest Hits
C&W 10/7/00 George Strait
C&W 11/24/01 The Road Less Traveled
C&W 6/28/03 Honkytonkville

STREISAND, Barbra
Pop 10/31/64 People
Pop 3/16/74 The Way We Were
Pop 2/12/77 A Star Is Born
Pop 1/6/79 Barbra Streisand's Greatest Hits, Volume 2
Pop 10/25/80 Guilty
Pop 1/25/86 The Broadway Album
Pop 7/17/93 Back To Broadway
Pop 11/29/97 Higher Ground

STUDDARD, Ruben
Pop 12/27/03 Soulful
R&B 1/31/04 ↓

STYX
Pop 4/4/81 Paradise Theater

SUMAC, Yma
Pop 4/7/51 Voice Of The Xtabay

SUMMER, Donna
Pop 11/11/78 Live And More
Pop 6/16/79 Bad Girls
R&B 6/23/79 ↓
Pop 1/5/80 On The Radio- Greatest Hits- Volumes I & II

SUPERTRAMP
Pop 5/19/79 Breakfast In America

SUPREMES, The
R&B 1/30/65 Where Did Our Love Go
R&B 4/23/66 I Hear A Symphony
Pop 10/22/66 The Supremes A' Go-Go
R&B 10/22/66 ↓
R&B 3/11/67 The Supremes sing Holland-Dozier-Holland
R&B 10/14/67 Diana Ross and the Supremes Greatest Hits
Pop 10/28/67 ↓
R&B 12/21/68 Diana Ross & The Supremes Join the Temptations
R&B 1/18/69 TCB
DIANA ROSS & THE SUPREMES with THE TEMPTATIONS
Pop 2/8/69 ↓

SWAN, Billy
C&W 1/18/75 I Can Help

SWEAT, Keith
R&B 3/19/88 Make It Last Forever
R&B 8/25/90 I'll Give All My Love To You
R&B 2/1/92 Keep It Comin'
R&B 7/16/94 Get Up On It
R&B 7/13/96 Keith Sweat

SYSTEM OF A DOWN
Pop 9/22/01 Toxicity

T

TANK
R&B 3/31/01 Force Of Nature

TAYLOR, Johnnie
R&B 4/10/76 Eargasm

TEARS FOR FEARS
Pop 7/13/85 Songs From The Big Chair

TEMPTATIONS, The
R&B 4/10/65 The Temptations Sing Smokey
R&B 12/11/65 Temptin' Temptations
R&B 7/30/66 Gettin' Ready
R&B 12/31/66 The Temptations Greatest Hits
R&B 4/8/67 Temptations Live!
R&B 9/2/67 With A Lot O' Soul
R&B 1/6/68 The Temptations in a Mellow Mood
R&B 6/22/68 Wish It Would Rain
R&B 12/21/68 Diana Ross & The Supremes Join the Temptations
R&B 1/18/69 TCB
DIANA ROSS & THE SUPREMES with THE TEMPTATIONS
Pop 2/8/69 ↓
R&B 3/29/69 Cloud Nine
R&B 11/1/69 Puzzle People
R&B 4/18/70 Psychedelic Shack
R&B 3/4/72 Solid Rock
R&B 11/25/72 All Directions
R&B 4/28/73 Masterpiece
R&B 5/3/75 A Song For You

THREE SUNS, The
Pop 5/15/48 Busy Fingers

TIFFANY
Pop 1/23/88 Tiffany

TLC
Pop 3/13/99 Fanmail
R&B 3/13/99 ↓

TONE LOC
Pop 4/15/89 Loc-ed After Dark

TOOL
Pop 6/2/01 Lateralus

TOO $HORT
R&B 11/13/93 Get In Where You Fit In
R&B 2/11/95 Cocktails
R&B 6/8/96 Gettin' It (Album Number Ten)
R&B 7/31/99 Can't Stay Away

TRAVIS, Randy
C&W 8/9/86 Storms Of Life
C&W 6/20/87 Always & Forever
C&W 8/27/88 Old 8x10
C&W 11/4/89 No Holdin' Back
C&W 11/24/90 Heroes And Friends

TRESVANT, Ralph
R&B 4/6/91 Ralph Tresvant

TRIBE CALLED QUEST, A
R&B 11/27/93 Midnight Marauders
Pop 8/17/96 Beats, Rhymes And Life
R&B 8/17/96 ↓

TUCKER, Tanya
C&W 11/6/76 Here's Some Love

TURNER, Tina
R&B 7/21/84 Private Dancer

TWAIN, Shania
C&W 7/22/95 The Woman In Me
C&W 11/22/97 Come On Over
Pop 12/7/02 Up!
C&W 12/7/02 ↓

TWISTA
Pop 2/14/04 Kamikaze
R&B 2/14/04 ↓

TWITTY, Conway
C&W 10/3/70 Hello Darlin'
C&W 9/15/73 Louisiana Woman- Mississippi Man
CONWAY TWITTY-LORETTA LYNN
C&W 10/6/73 You've Never Been This Far Before/ Baby's Gone
C&W 6/1/74 Conway Twitty's Honky Tonk Angel

TWITTY, Conway — Cont'd

C&W	9/21/74	Country Partners **LORETTA LYNN/CONWAY TWITTY**
C&W	3/15/75	Linda On My Mind
C&W	8/16/75	Feelins'
C&W	8/7/76	United Talent **LORETTA LYNN/CONWAY TWITTY** (above 2)
C&W	1/8/77	Conway Twitty's Greatest Hits Vol. II

2PAC

Pop	4/1/95	Me Against The World
R&B	4/1/95	↓
Pop	3/2/96	All Eyez On Me
R&B	3/2/96	↓
Pop	11/23/96	The Don Killuminati - The 7 Day Theory **MAKAVELI**
R&B	11/23/96	↓
R&B	12/13/97	R U Still Down? [Remember Me]
R&B	12/12/98	Greatest Hits
Pop	4/14/01	Until The End Of Time
R&B	4/14/01	↓
R&B	12/14/02	Better Dayz

U

USA FOR AFRICA

Pop	4/27/85	We Are The World

USHER

R&B	1/10/98	My Way

U2

Pop	4/25/87	The Joshua Tree
Pop	11/12/88	Rattle And Hum
Pop	12/7/91	Achtung Baby
Pop	7/24/93	Zooropa
Pop	3/22/97	Pop

V

VANDROSS, Luther

R&B	11/14/81	Never Too Much
R&B	11/6/82	Forever, For Always, For Love
R&B	4/14/84	Busy Body
R&B	5/4/85	The Night I Fell In Love
R&B	11/29/86	Give Me The Reason
R&B	11/26/88	Any Love
R&B	6/22/91	Power Of Love
Pop	6/28/03	Dance With My Father
R&B	6/28/03	↓

VANGELIS

Pop	4/17/82	Chariots Of Fire

VAN HALEN

Pop	4/26/86	5150
Pop	6/25/88	OU812
Pop	7/6/91	For Unlawful Carnal Knowledge
Pop	2/11/95	Balance
Pop	11/9/96	Best Of Volume 1

VANILLA ICE

Pop	11/10/90	To The Extreme

VAUGHN, Billy

Pop	5/2/60	Theme from A Summer Place

W

WALKER, Jr., & The All Stars

R&B	7/24/65	Shotgun

WALLACE, Jerry

C&W	9/9/72	To Get To You
C&W	12/8/73	Primrose Lane/Don't Give Up On Me

WAR

R&B	2/10/73	The World Is A Ghetto
Pop	2/17/73	↓
R&B	9/22/73	Deliver The Word
R&B	6/22/74	War Live!
R&B	8/30/75	Why Can't We Be Friends?

WARREN G

R&B	6/25/94	Regulate...G Funk Era

WARWICK, Dionne

R&B	7/29/67	Here Where There is Love

WASHINGTON, Grover Jr.

R&B	5/17/75	Mister Magic
R&B	12/20/75	Feels So Good

WASHINGTON, Keith

R&B	7/6/91	Make Time For Love

WATLEY, Jody

R&B	6/6/87	Jody Watley

WELK, Lawrence

Pop	3/13/61	Calcutta!

WEST, Dottie — see ROGERS, Kenny

WEST, Kanye

R&B	2/28/04	The College Dropout

WESTSIDE CONNECTION

R&B	11/9/96	Bow Down

WHISPERS, The

R&B	2/23/80	The Whispers
R&B	4/17/82	Love Is Where You Find It

WHITE, Barry

R&B	7/7/73	I've Got So Much To Give
R&B	2/2/74	Stone Gon'
Pop	10/26/74	Can't Get Enough
R&B	11/23/74	↓
R&B	5/31/75	Just Another Way To Say I Love You
R&B	10/15/77	Barry White Sings For Someone You Love
R&B	11/25/78	Barry White The Man
R&B	11/26/94	The Icon Is Love

WHITE, Karyn

R&B	1/28/89	Karyn White

WILD CHERRY

R&B	9/11/76	Wild Cherry

WILLIAMS, Andy

Pop	5/4/63	Days of Wine and Roses

WILLIAMS, Don

C&W	6/26/76	Harmony

WILLIAMS, Hank Jr.

C&W	7/5/69	Songs My Father Left Me
C&W	7/21/84	Major Moves
C&W	6/22/85	Five-O
C&W	2/8/86	Greatest Hits - Volume 2
C&W	9/6/86	Montana Cafe
C&W	4/11/87	Hank "Live"
C&W	8/29/87	Born To Boogie
C&W	8/13/88	Wild Streak
C&W	4/1/89	Greatest Hits III

WILLIAMS, Vanessa

R&B	5/2/92	The Comfort Zone

WINANS, BeBe & CeCe

R&B	10/26/91	Different Lifestyles

WINWOOD, Steve

Pop	8/20/88	Roll With It

WITHERS, Bill

R&B	7/15/72	Still Bill

WOMACK, Bobby

R&B	2/20/82	The Poet

WOMACK, Lee Ann

C&W	6/10/00	I Hope You Dance

WONDER, Stevie

Pop	8/24/63	Little Stevie Wonder/ The 12 Year Old Genius
R&B	1/20/73	Talking Book
R&B	9/8/73	Innervisions
Pop	9/14/74	Fulfillingness' First Finale
R&B	10/5/74	↓
Pop	10/16/76	Songs In The Key Of Life
R&B	10/16/76	↓
R&B	11/22/80	Hotter Than July
R&B	6/5/82	Stevie Wonder's Original Musiquarium I
R&B	12/8/84	The Woman In Red
R&B	11/9/85	In Square Circle
R&B	12/19/87	Characters
R&B	8/3/91	Music From The Movie Jungle Fever

WORLEY, Darryl

C&W	8/3/02	I Miss My Friend
C&W	5/3/03	Have You Forgotten?

WU-TANG CLAN

Pop	6/21/97	Wu-Tang Forever
R&B	6/21/97	↓
R&B	12/9/00	The W

WYNETTE, Tammy

C&W	9/21/68	D-I-V-O-R-C-E
C&W	7/25/70	Tammy's Touch
C&W	10/30/76	Golden Ring **GEORGE JONES & TAMMY WYNETTE**

WYNONNA

C&W	4/18/92	Wynonna
C&W	5/29/93	Tell Me Why
C&W	8/23/03	What The World Needs Now Is Love

X

XZIBIT

R&B	12/30/00	Restless
R&B	10/19/02	Man vs Machine

Y

YARBROUGH & PEOPLES
R&B 3/7/81 The Two Of Us

YEARWOOD, Trisha
C&W 9/13/97 Songbook - A Collection Of Hits
C&W 6/23/01 Inside Out

YOAKAM, Dwight
C&W 6/28/86 Guitars, Cadillacs, Etc., Etc.
C&W 6/6/87 Hillbilly Deluxe
C&W 10/22/88 Buenas Noches From A Lonely Room

YOUNG, Neil
Pop 3/11/72 Harvest

YOUNG BLEED
R&B 2/7/98 All I Have In This World, Are...My Balls And My Word

YOUNGBLOODZ
R&B 9/27/03 Drankin' Patnaz

YOUNG GUNZ
R&B 3/13/04 Tough Luv

Z

ZAPP
R&B 10/25/80 Zapp

SOUNDTRACKS

R&B 4/9/94 Above The Rim
Pop 1/12/52 American In Paris, An
Pop 8/12/50 Annie Get Your Gun
Pop 7/18/98 Armageddon
Pop 7/22/57 Around The World In 80 Days
Pop 8/2/03 Bad Boys II
R&B 8/2/03 ↓
Pop 6/22/85 Beverly Hills Cop
R&B 8/8/92 Boomerang
R&B 9/7/91 Boyz N The Hood
Pop 5/6/50 Cinderella
Pop 6/13/98 City Of Angels
C&W 8/26/00 Coyote Ugly
Pop 6/4/94 Crow, The
Pop 9/2/95 Dangerous Minds
R&B 11/4/95 Dead Presidents
Pop 3/17/73 Deliverance
C&W 3/17/73 ↓
Pop 11/14/87 Dirty Dancing
Pop 11/5/66 Doctor Zhivago
Pop 10/13/56 Eddy Duchin Story, The
Pop 11/16/02 8 Mile
R&B 11/16/02 ↓
Pop 1/23/61 Exodus
Pop 6/25/83 Flashdance
Pop 4/21/84 Footloose
R&B 4/29/95 Friday
Pop 5/13/95 ↓
R&B 10/25/97 Gang Related
Pop 7/21/58 Gigi
Pop 3/20/65 Goldfinger
Pop 7/29/78 Grease
Pop 2/15/97 Gridlock'd
R&B 2/15/97 ↓
C&W 6/20/98 Hope Floats
R&B 4/25/98 I Got The Hook-Up!
R&B 6/7/97 I'm Bout It
R&B 10/29/94 Jason's Lyric
Pop 10/6/56 King And I, The
Pop 7/16/94 Lion King, The
Pop 3/13/65 Mary Poppins
Pop 7/26/97 Men In Black - The Album
R&B 6/26/93 Menace II Society
Pop 10/18/52 Merry Widow, The
Pop 11/5/94 Murder Was The Case
R&B 11/5/94 ↓
R&B 4/27/91 New Jack City
R&B 6/29/96 Nutty Professor, The
R&B 7/29/00 Nutty Professor II: The Klumps
C&W 2/24/01 O Brother, Where Art Thou?
Pop 3/23/02 ↓
Pop 1/28/56 Oklahoma!
Pop 7/22/95 Pocahontas
Pop 3/15/97 Private Parts
R&B 2/1/97 Rhyme & Reason
R&B 4/15/00 Romeo Must Die
R&B 9/2/95 Show, The
Pop 8/11/51 Show Boat
Pop 8/21/93 Sleepless In Seattle
R&B 10/18/97 Soul Food
Pop 11/13/65 Sound Of Music, The
Pop 5/19/58 South Pacific
Pop 2/21/53 Stars And Stripes Forever
R&B 2/16/02 State Property

R&B 5/11/96 Sunset Park
R&B 6/10/95 Tales From The Hood
Pop 9/30/50 Three Little Words
Pop 1/24/98 Titanic
R&B 6/21/03 2 Fast 2 Furious
Pop 7/26/86 Top Gun
C&W 8/2/80 Urban Cowboy
R&B 12/16/95 Waiting To Exhale
Pop 1/20/96 ↓
R&B 3/31/73 Wattstax: The Living Word
Pop 4/4/92 Wayne's World
Pop 5/5/62 West Side Story
Pop 7/11/70 Woodstock
Pop 2/12/49 Words And Music

ORIGINAL CASTS

Pop 6/5/61 Camelot
Pop 7/17/61 Carnival
Pop 8/11/45 Carousel
Pop 2/2/59 Flower Drum Song
Pop 3/17/51 Guys And Dolls
Pop 4/26/69 Hair
Pop 6/6/64 Hello, Dolly!
Pop 3/19/49 Kiss Me, Kate
Pop 3/17/58 Music Man, The
Pop 7/14/56 My Fair Lady
Pop 4/14/45 Song of Norway
Pop 1/25/60 Sound Of Music, The
Pop 6/4/49 South Pacific

TV SOUNDTRACK

Pop 11/2/85 Miami Vice

VARIOUS ARTIST COMPILATIONS

C&W 11/6/93 Common Thread: The Songs Of The Eagles
Pop 11/3/01 God Bless America
Pop 2/20/71 Jesus Christ Superstar
Pop 9/6/03 Neptunes Present... Clones, The
R&B 9/6/03 ↓
Pop 8/5/00 Now 4
Pop 4/21/01 Now 6
Pop 8/18/01 Now 7
Pop 4/6/02 Now 9
Pop 6/1/02 P. Diddy & Bad Boy Records Present... We Invented The Remix
C&W 3/26/94 Rhythm Country And Blues
Pop 7/17/61 Stars For A Summer Night
R&B 8/30/03 State Property Presents: The Chain Gang Vol. II
Pop 10/16/48 Theme Songs
R&B 8/28/99 Violator - The Album

RECORD RESEARCH BOOKS

In addition to *#1 Album Pix 1945-2003*, Joel Whitburn authors many other Billboard chart books. Please call, write or visit our Web site to receive further information. A catalog is available upon request.

☎ **U.S. Toll-Free**:   **1-800-827-9810**
(orders only please – Mon-Fri 8 AM-12 PM, 1 PM-5 PM CST)

Foreign Orders: 1-262-251-5408

Questions?:   1-262-251-5408 or **Email**: books@recordresearch.com

💻 **Online at our Web site**: www.recordresearch.com

▤ **Fax** (24 hours):   1-262-251-9452

📪 **Mail**: Record Research Inc.
P.O. Box 200
Menomonee Falls, WI 53052-0200
U.S.A.

Payments methods accepted: MasterCard, VISA, American Express, Check, or Money Order.

Shipping/Handling Extra — If you do not order through our online Web site (see above), please contact us for shipping rates.

U.S. orders are shipped via UPS (please provide complete street address); please allow 7-10 business days for delivery.

Canadian and **Foreign** orders are shipped via surface mail (book rate); please allow **8-12 weeks for delivery**. Orders must be paid in US. dollars and drawn on a U.S. bank.

For faster delivery, contact us for other shipping options/rates.